MW01118198

“Are

yours?” Danzig yelled. “Come back before you get yourselves killed!”

“Will you dry up?” Scobie snarled over the radio. “It’s nothing but a style of talk we’ve got between us. If you can’t understand that, you’ve got less of a brain than we do.”

“Listen, won’t you? I didn’t say you’re crazy. You don’t have delusions or anything like that. I do say you’ve steered your fantasies toward this kind of place, and now the reality has reinforced them till you’re under a compulsion you don’t recognize. Would you go ahead so recklessly anywhere else in the universe? Think!”

“That does it. We’ll resume contact after you’ve had time to improve your manners.” Scobie snapped off his main radio switch. The circuits that stayed active served for close-by communications but had no power to reach an orbital relay. His companion did likewise.

The three faced the awesomeness of Iapetus before them.

“You can help me find the Princess when we are inside, Alvarlan,” *Kendrick says.*

“That I can and will,” *the sorcerer vows.*

“I wait for you, most steadfast of my lovers,” *Ricia croons.*

Alone in the spacecraft above, Danzig well-nigh sobbed, “Oh, damn that game forever!” The sound fell away into emptiness.

The Tor SF Doubles

A Meeting with Medusa/Green Mars, Arthur C. Clarke/Kim Stanley Robinson • **Hardfought/Cascade Point,** Greg Bear/Timothy Zahn • **Born with the Dead/The Saliva Tree,** Robert Silverberg/Brian W. Aldiss • **No Truce with Kings/Ship of Shadows,** Poul Anderson/Fritz Leiber • **Enemy Mine/Another Orphan,** Barry B. Longyear/John Kessel • **Screwtop/The Girl Who Was Plugged In,** Vonda N. McIntyre/James Tiptree, Jr. • **The Nemesis from Terra/Battle for the Stars,** Leigh Brackett/Edmond Hamilton • **The Ugly Little Boy/The [Widget], the [Wadget], and Boff,** Isaac Asimov/Theodore Sturgeon • **Sailing to Byzantium/Seven American Nights,** Robert Silverberg/Gene Wolfe • **Houston, Houston, Do You Read?/Souls,** James Tiptree, Jr./Joanna Russ • **He Who Shapes/The Infinity Box,** Roger Zelazny/Kate Wilhelm • **The Blind Geometer/The New Atlantis,** Kim Stanley Robinson/Ursula K. Le Guin • **The Saturn Game/Iceborn,** Poul Anderson/Gregory Benford and Paul A. Carter • **The Last Castle/Nightwings,*** Jack Vance/Robert Silverberg • **The Color of Neanderthal Eyes/And Strange at Ecbatan the Trees,*** James Tiptree, Jr./Michael Bishop • **Divide and Rule/The Sword of Rhiannon,*** L. Sprague de Camp/Leigh Brackett

**forthcoming*

POUL ANDERSON

A TOM DOHERTY ASSOCIATES BOOK
NEW YORK

This is a work of fiction. All the characters and events portrayed in this book are fictitious, and any resemblance to real people or events is purely coincidental.

THE SATURN GAME

Copyright © 1981 by Ziff-Davis Publishing Corporation, Inc.; copyright © 1981, 1989 by Poul Anderson

All rights reserved, including the right to reproduce this book or portions thereof in any form.

A TOR Book
Published by Tom Doherty Associates, Inc.
49 West 24 Street
New York, NY 10010

Cover photograph courtesy of NASA

ISBN: 0-812-50277-9   Can. ISBN: 0-812-50269-8

First edition: November 1989

Printed in the United States of America

0 9 8 7 6 5 4 3 2 1

I

If we would understand what happened, which is vital if we would avoid repeated and worse tragedies in the future, we must begin by dismissing all accusations. Nobody was negligent; no action was foolish. For who could have predicted the eventuality, or recognized its nature, until too late? Rather should we appreciate the spirit with which those people struggled against disaster, inward and outward, after they knew. The fact is that thresholds exist throughout reality, and that things on their far sides are altogether different from things on their hither sides. The *Chronos* crossed more than an abyss, it crossed a threshold of human experience.

—Francis L. Minamoto,
Death Under Saturn: A Dissenting View
(Apollo University Communications,
Leyburg, Luna, 2057)

"The City of Ice is now on my horizon," *Kendrick says. Its towers gleam blue.* "My griffin spreads his wings to glide." *Wind whistles among those great, rainbow-shimmering pinions. His cloak blows back from his shoulders; the air strikes through his ring-mail and sheathes him in cold.* "I lean over and peer after you." *The spear in his left hand counterbalances him. Its head flickers palely with the moonlight that Wayland Smith hammered into the steel.*

"Yes, I see the griffin," *Ricia tells him,* "high and far, like a comet above the courtyard walls. I run out from under the portico for a better look. A guard tries to stop me, grabs my sleeve, but I tear the spider-silk apart and dash forth into the open." *The elven castle wavers as if its sculptured ice were turning to smoke. Passionately, she cries,* "Is it in truth you, my darling?"

"Hold, there!" *warns Alvarlan from his cave of arcana ten thousand leagues away.* "I send your mind the message that if the King suspects this is Sir Kendrick of the Isles, he will raise a dragon against him, or spirit you off beyond any chance of rescue. Go back, Princess of Maranoa. Pretend you decide that it is only an eagle. I will cast a belief-spell on your words."

"I stay far aloft," *Kendrick says.* "Save he use a scrying stone, the Elf King will not be aware this beast has a rider. From here I'll spy out city and castle." *And then—? He knows not. He knows simply that he must set her free or die in the quest. How long will it take him, how many more nights will she lie in the King's embrace?*

"I thought you were supposed to spy out Iapetus," Mark Danzig interrupted.

His dry tone startled the three others into alertness. Jean Broberg flushed with embarrassment, Colin Scobie with irritation; Luis Garcilaso shrugged, grinned, and turned his gaze to the pilot console before which he sat harnessed. For a moment silence filled the cabin, and shadows, and radiance from the universe.

To help observation, all lights were out except a few dim glows at instruments. The sunward ports were lidded. Elsewhere thronged stars, so many and so brilliant that they wellnigh drowned the blackness which held them. The Milky Way was a torrent of silver. One port framed Saturn at half phase, dayside pale gold and rich bands amidst the jewelry of its rings, nightside wanly ashimmer with starlight and moonlight upon clouds, as big to the sight as Earth over Luna.

Forward was Iapetus. The spacecraft rotated while orbiting the moon, to maintain a steady optical field. It had crossed the dawn line, presently at the middle of the inward-facing hemisphere. Thus it had left bare, crater-pocked land behind it in the dark, and was passing above sunlit glacier country. Whiteness dazzled, glittered in sparks and shards of color, reached fantastic shapes heavenward; cirques, crevasses, caverns brimmed with blue.

"I'm sorry," Jean Broberg whispered. "It's too beautiful, unbelievably beautiful, and . . .

almost like the place where our game had brought us—Took us by surprise—"

"Huh!" Mark Danzig said. "You had a pretty good idea of what to expect, therefore you made your play go in the direction of something that resembled it. Don't tell me any different. I've watched these acts for eight years."

Colin Scobie made a savage gesture. Spin and gravity were too slight to give noticeable weight. His movement sent him through the air, across the crowded cabin, until he checked himself by a handhold just short of the chemist. "Are you calling Jean a liar?" he growled.

Most times he was cheerful, in a bluff fashion. Perhaps because of that, he suddenly appeared menacing. He was a big, sandy-haired man in his mid-thirties; a coverall did not disguise the muscles beneath, and the scowl on his face brought forth its ruggedness.

"Please!" Broberg exclaimed. "Not a quarrel, Colin."

The geologist glanced back at her. She was slender and fine-featured. At her age of forty-two, despite longevity treatment, the reddish-brown hair that fell to her shoulders was becoming streaked with white, and lines were engraved around large gray eyes. "Mark is right," she sighed. "We're here to do science, not daydream." She reached forth to touch Scobie's arm, smiled shyly. "You're still full of your Kendrick persona, aren't you? Gallant, protective—" She stopped. Her voice had quickened with more than a hint of Ricia. She covered her lips and flushed again. A tear broke free and sparkled off on air currents. She forced a laugh.

"But I'm just physicist Broberg, wife of astronomer Tom, mother of Johnnie and Billy."

Her glance went Saturnward, as if seeking the ship where her family waited. She might have spied it, too, as a star that moved among stars, by the solar sail. However, that was now furled, and naked vision could not find even such huge hulls as *Chronos* possessed, across millions of kilometers.

Luis Garcilaso asked from his pilot's chair: "What harm if we carry on our little *commedia dell' arte*?" His Arizona drawl soothed the ear. "We won't be landin' for a while yet, and everything's on automatic till then." He was small, swart, deft, still in his twenties.

Danzig twisted the leather of his countenance into a frown. At sixty, thanks to his habits as well as to longevity, he kept springiness in a lank frame; he could joke about wrinkles and encroaching baldness. In this hour, he set humor aside.

"Do you mean you don't know what's the matter?" His beak of a nose pecked at a scanner screen which magnified the moonscape. "Almighty God! That's a new world we're about to touch down on—tiny, but a world, and strange in ways we can't guess. Nothing's been here before us except one unmanned flyby and one unmanned lander that soon quit sending. We can't rely on meters and cameras alone. We've got to use our eyes and brains." He addressed Scobie. "You should realize that in your bones, Colin, if nobody else aboard does. You've worked on Luna as well as Earth. In spite of all the settlements, in spite of all the study that's been done, did you never hit any nasty surprises?"

The burly man had recovered his temper. Into his own voice came a softness that recalled the serenity of the Idaho mountains whence he hailed. "True," he admitted. "There's no such thing as having too much information when you're off Earth, or enough information, for that matter." He paused. "Nevertheless, timidity can be as dangerous as rashness—not that you're timid, Mark," he added in haste. "Why, you and Rachel could've been in a nice O'Neill on a nice pension—"

Danzig relaxed and smiled. "This was a challenge, if I may sound pompous. Just the same, we want to get home when we're finished here. We should be in time for the Bar Mitzvah of a great-grandson or two. Which requires staying alive."

"My point is, if you let yourself get buffaloed, you may end up in a worse bind than— Oh, never mind. You're probably right, and we should not have begun fantasizing. The spectacle sort of grabbed us. It won't happen again."

Yet when Scobie's eyes looked anew on the glacier, they had not quite the dispassion of a scientist in them. Nor did Broberg's or Garcilaso's. Danzig slammed fist into palm. "The game, the damned childish game," he muttered, too low for his companions to hear. "Was nothing saner possible for them?"

II

Was nothing saner possible for them? Perhaps not.

If we are to answer the question, we should first review some history. When early industrial operations in space offered the hope of rescuing civilization, and Earth, from ruin, then greater knowledge of sister planets, prior to their development, became a clear necessity. The effort must start with Mars, the least hostile. No natural law forbade sending small manned spacecraft yonder. What did was the absurdity of as much fuel, time, and effort as were required, in order that three or four persons might spend a few days in a single locality.

Construction of the *J. Peter Vajk* took longer and cost more, but paid off when it, virtually a colony, spread its immense solar sail and took a thousand people to their goal in half a year and in comparative comfort. The payoff grew overwhelming when they, from orbit, launched Earthward the beneficiated minerals of Phobos that they did not need for their own purposes. Those purposes, of course, turned on the truly thorough, long-term study of Mars, and included landings of auxiliary craft, for ever lengthier stays, all over the surface.

Sufficient to remind you of this much; no need to detail the triumphs of the same basic concept throughout the inner Solar System, as far as Jupiter. The tragedy of the *Vladimir* became a reason to try again for Mercury . . . and, in a left-handed, political way, pushed the Britannic-American consortium into its *Chronos* project.

They named the ship better than they knew. Sailing time to Saturn was eight years.

Not only the scientists must be healthy, lively-minded people. Crewfolk, technicians, medics, constables, teachers, clergy, entertainers, every element of an entire community must be. Each must command more than a single skill, for emergency backup, and keep those skills alive by regular, tedious rehearsal. The environment was limited and austere; communication with home was soon a matter of beamcasts; cosmopolitans found themselves in what amounted to an isolated village. What were they to *do*?

Assigned tasks. Civic projects, especially work on improving the interior of the vessel. Research, or writing a book, or the study of a subject, or sports, or hobby clubs, or service and handicraft enterprises, or more private interactions, or—There was a wide choice of television tapes, but Central Control made sets usable for only three hours in twenty-four. You dared not get into the habit of passivity.

Individuals grumbled, squabbled, formed and dissolved cliques, formed and dissolved marriages or less explicit relationships, begot and raised occasional children, worshipped, mocked, learned, yearned, and for the most part found reasonable satisfaction in life. But for some, including a large proportion of the gifted, what made the difference between this and misery was their psychodramas.

—Minamoto

Dawn crept past the ice, out onto the rock. It was a light both dim and harsh, yet sufficient to give Garcilaso the last data he wanted for descent.

The hiss of the motor died away, a thump shivered through the hull, landing jacks leveled it, stillness fell. The crew did not speak for a while. They were staring out at Iapetus.

Immediately around them was desolation like that which reigns in much of the Solar System. A darkling plain curved visibly away to a horizon that, at man-height, was a bare three kilometers distant; higher up in the cabin, you saw farther, but that only sharpened the sense of being on a minute ball awhirl among the stars. The ground was thinly covered with cosmic dust and gravel; here and there a minor crater or an upthrust mass lifted out of the regolith to cast long, knife-edged, utterly black shadows. Light reflections lessened the number of visible stars, turning heaven into a bowlful of night. Halfway between the zenith and the south, half-Saturn and its rings made the vista beautiful.

Likewise did the glacier—or the glaciers? Nobody was sure. The sole knowledge was that, seen from afar, Iapetus gleamed bright at the western end of its orbit and grew dull at the eastern end, because one side was covered with whitish material while the other side was not; the dividing line passed nearly beneath the planet which it eternally faced. The probes from *Chronos* had reported the layer was thick, with puzzling spectra that varied from place to place, and little more about it.

In this hour, four humans gazed across pitted emptiness and saw wonder rear over the world-rim. From north to south went ramparts, battlements, spires, depths, peaks, cliffs, their shapes and shadings an infinity of fantasies. On the right Saturn cast soft amber, but that was nearly lost in the glare from the east, where a sun dwarfed almost to stellar size nonetheless blazed too fierce to look at, just above the summit. There the silvery sheen exploded in brilliance, diamond-glitter of shattered light, chill blues and greens; dazzled to tears, eyes saw the vision glimmer and waver, as if it bordered on dreamland, or on Faerie. But despite all delicate intricacies, underneath was a sense of chill and of brutal mass; here dwelt also the Frost Giants.

Broberg was the first to breathe forth a word. "The City of Ice."

"Magic," said Garcilaso as low. "My spirit could lose itself forever, wanderin' yonder. I'm not sure I'd mind. My cave is nothin' like this, nothin'—"

"Wait a minute!" snapped Danzig in alarm.

"Oh, yes. Curb the imagination, please." Though Scobie was quick to utter sobrieties, they sounded drier than needful. "We know from probe transmissions the scarp is, well, Grand Canyon-like. Sure, it's more spectacular than we realized, which I suppose makes it still more of a mystery." He turned to Broberg. "I've never seen ice or snow as sculptured as this. Have you, Jean? You've mentioned visiting a lot of mountain and winter scenery when you were a girl in Canada."

The physicist shook her head. "No. Never. It doesn't seem possible. What could have done it? There's no weather here . . . is there?"

"Perhaps the same phenomenon is responsible that laid a hemisphere bare," Danzig suggested.

"Or that covered a hemisphere," Scobie said. "An object seventeen hundred kilometers across shouldn't have gases, frozen or otherwise. Unless it's a ball of such stuff clear through, like a comet. Which we know it's not." As if to demonstrate, he unclipped a pair of pliers from a nearby tool rack, tossed it, and caught it on its slow way down. His own ninety kilos of mass weighed about seven. For that, the satellite must be essentially rocky.

Garcilaso registered impatience. "Let's stop tradin' facts and theories we already know about, and start findin' answers."

Rapture welled in Broberg. "Yes, let's get out. Over *there*."

"Hold on," protested Danzig as Garcilaso and Scobie nodded eagerly. "You can't be serious. Caution, step-by-step advance—"

"No, it's too wonderful for that." Broberg's tone shivered.

"Yeah, to hell with fiddlin' around," Garcilaso said. "We need at least a preliminary scout right away."

The furrows deepened in Danzig's visage. "You mean you, too, Luis? But you're our pilot!"

"On the ground I'm general assistant, chief cook, and bottle washer to you scientists. Do you imagine I want to sit idle, with somethin' like that to explore?" Garcilaso calmed his voice. "Besides, if I should come to grief, any of you can fly back, given a bit of radio talk from *Chronos* and a final approach under remote control."

"It's quite reasonable, Mark," Scobie argued. "Contrary to doctrine, true; but doctrine was made for us, not vice versa. A short distance, low gravity, and we'll be on the lookout for hazards. The point is, until we have some notion of what that ice is like, we don't know what the devil to pay attention to in this vicinity, either. No, we'll take a quick jaunt. When we return, then we'll plan."

Danzig stiffened. "May I remind you, if anything goes wrong, help is at least a hundred hours away? An auxiliary like this can't boost any higher if it's to get back, and it'd take longer than that to disengage the big boats from Saturn and Titan."

Scobie reddened at the implied insult. "And

may I remind you, on the ground I am the captain? I say an immediate reconnaissance is safe and desirable. Stay behind if you want—In fact, yes, you must. Doctrine is right in saying the vessel mustn't be deserted."

Danzig studied him for several seconds before murmuring, "Luis goes, however, is that it?"

"Yes!" cried Garcilaso so that the cabin rang.

Broberg patted Danzig's limp hand. "It's okay, Mark," she said gently. "We'll bring back samples for you to study. After that, I wouldn't be surprised but what the best ideas about procedure will be yours."

He shook his head. Suddenly he looked very tired. "No," he replied in a monotone, "that won't happen. You see, I'm only a hardnosed industrial chemist who saw this expedition as a chance to do interesting research. The whole way through space, I kept myself busy with ordinary affairs, including, you remember, a couple of inventions I'd wanted leisure to develop. You three, you're younger, you're romantics—"

"Aw, come off it, Mark." Scobie tried to laugh. "Maybe Jean and Luis are, a little, but me, I'm about as other-worldly as a plate of haggis."

"You played the game, year after year, until at last the game started playing you. That's what's going on this minute, no matter how you rationalize your motives." Danzig's gaze on the geologist, who was his friend, lost the defiance that had been in it and turned wistful. "You might try recalling Delia Ames."

Scobie bristled. "What about her? The business was hers and mine, nobody else's."

"Except afterward she cried on Rachel's shoulder, and Rachel doesn't keep secrets from me. Don't worry, I'm not about to blab. Anyhow, Delia got over it. But if you'd recollect objectively, you'd see what had happened to you, already three years ago."

Scobie set his jaw. Danzig smiled in the left corner of his mouth. "No, I suppose you can't," he went on. "I admit I'd no idea either, till now, how far the process had gone. At least keep your fantasies in the background while you're outside, will you? Can you?"

In half a decade of travel, Scobie's apartment had become idiosyncratically his—perhaps more so than was usual, since he remained a bachelor who seldom had women visitors for longer than a few nightwatches at a time. Much of the furniture he had made himself; the agrosections of *Chronos* produced wood, hide, fiber as well as food and fresh air. His handiwork ran to massiveness and archaic carved decorations. Most of what he wanted to read he screened from the data banks, of course, but a shelf held a few old books, Childe's border ballads, an eighteenth-century family Bible (despite his agnosticism), a copy of *The Machinery of Freedom* which had nearly disintegrated but displayed the signature of the author, and other valued miscellany. Above them stood a model of a sailboat in which he had cruised Northern European waters, and a trophy he had won in handball aboard this ship. On the bulkheads hung his fencing sabers and numerous pictures—of parents and siblings, of wilderness areas he had tramped on Earth, of castles and mountains and heaths in Scotland where he had often been too, of his geological team on Luna, of Thomas Jefferson and, imagined, Robert the Bruce.

On a certain evenwatch he had, though, been seated before his telescreen. Lights were turned low in order that he might fully savor the image. Auxiliary craft were out in a joint exercise, and a couple of their personnel used the opportunity to beam back views of what they saw.

That was splendor. Starful space made a chalice for *Chronos*. The two huge, majestically counter-rotating cylinders, the entire complex of linkages, ports, locks, shields, collectors, transmitters, docks, all became Japanesely exquisite at a distance of several hundred kilometers. It was the solar sail which filled most of the screen, like a turning golden sun-wheel; yet remote vision could also appreciate its spiderweb intricacy, soaring and subtle curvatures, even the less-than-gossamer thinness. A mightier work than the Pyramids, a finer work than a refashioned chromosome, the ship moved on toward a Saturn which had become the second brightest beacon in the firmament.

The doorchime hauled Scobie out of his exaltation. As he started across the deck, he stubbed his toe on a table leg. Coriolis force caused that. It was slight, when a hull this size spun to give a full gee of weight, and a thing to which he had long since adapted; but now and then he got so interested in something that Terrestrial habits returned. He swore at his absent-mindedness, good-naturedly, since he anticipated a pleasurable time.

When he opened the door, Delia Ames entered in a single stride. At once she closed it behind her and stood braced against it. She was a tall blonde woman who did electronics maintenance and kept up a number of outside activities. "Hey!" Scobie said. "What's wrong? You look like—" he tried for levity—"something my cat wouldn've dragged in, if we had any mice or beached fish aboard."

She drew a ragged breath. Her Australian accent thickened till he had trouble understanding: "I . . . today . . . I happened to be at the same cafeteria table as George Harding—"

Unease tingled through Scobie. Harding worked in Ames' department but had much more in common with him. In the same group to which they both belonged, Harding likewise took a vaguely ancestral role, N'Kuma the Lionslayer.

"What happened?" Scobie asked.

Woe stared back at him. "He mentioned . . . you and he and the rest . . . you'd be taking your next holiday together . . . to carry on your, your bloody act uninterrupted."

"Well, yes. Work at the new park over in Starboard Hull will be suspended till enough metal's been recycled for the water pipes. The area will be vacant, and my gang has arranged to spend a week's worth of days—"

"But you and I were going to Lake Armstrong!"

"Uh, wait, that was just a notion we talked about, no definite plan yet, and this is such an unusual chance—Later, sweetheart. I'm sorry." He took her hands. They felt cold. He essayed a smile. "Now, c'mon, we were going to cook a festive dinner together and afterward spend a, shall we say, quiet evening at home. But for a start, this absolutely gorgeous presentation on the screen—"

She jerked free of him. The gesture seemed to calm her. "No, thanks," she said, flat-voiced. "Not when you'd rather be with that Broberg woman. I only came by to tell you in person I'm getting out of the way of you two."

"*Huh?*" He stepped back. "What the flaming hell do you mean?"

"You know jolly well."

"I don't! She, I, she's happily married, got two kids, she's older than me, we're friends, sure, but there's never been a thing between us that wasn't in the open and on the level—" Scobie swallowed. "You suppose maybe I'm in love with her?"

Ames looked away. Her fingers writhed together. "I'm not about to go on being a mere convenience to you, Colin. You have plenty of those. Myself, I'd hoped— But I was wrong, and I'm going to cut my losses before they get worse."

"But . . . Dee, I swear I haven't fallen for anybody else, and I, I swear you're more than a body to me, you're a fine person—" She stood mute and withdrawn. Scobie gnawed his lip before he could tell her: "Okay, I admit it, a main reason I volunteered for this trip was I'd lost out in a love affair on Earth. Not that the project doesn't interest me, but I've come to realize what a big chunk out of my life it is. You, more than any other woman, Dee, you've gotten me to feel better about the situation."

She grimaced. "But not as much as your psychodrama has, right?"

"Hey, you must think I'm obsessed with the game. I'm not. It's fun and—oh, maybe 'fun' is too weak a word—but anyhow, it's just little bunches of people getting together fairly regularly to play. Like my fencing, or a chess club, or, anything."

She squared her shoulders. "Well, then," she asked, "will you cancel the date you've made and spend your holiday with me?"

"I, uh, I can't do that. Not at this stage. Kendrick isn't off on the periphery of current events, he's closely involved with everybody else. If I didn't show, it'd spoil things for the rest."

Her glance steadied upon them. "Very well. A promise is a promise, or so I imagined. But afterward—Don't be afraid, I'm not trying to trap you. That would be no good, would it? However, if I maintain this liaison of ours, will you phase out of your game?"

"I can't—" Anger seized him. "No, God damn it!" he roared.

"Then goodbye, Colin," she said, and departed. He stared for minutes at the door she had shut behind her.

* * *

Unlike the large Titan and Saturn-vicinity explorers, landers on the airless moons were simply modified Luna-to-space shuttles, reliable but with limited capabilities. When the blocky shape had dropped below the horizon, Garcilaso said into his radio: "We've lost sight of the boat, Mark. I must say it improves the view." One of the relay micro-satellites which had been sown in orbit passed his words on.

"Better start blazing your trail, then," Danzig reminded.

"My, my, you *are* a fussbudget, aren't you?" Nevertheless Garcilaso unholstered the squirt gun at his hip and splashed a vividly fluorescent circle of paint on the ground. He would do it at eyeball intervals until his party reached the glacier. Except where dust lay thick over the regolith, footprints were faint, under the feeble gravity, and absent when a walker crossed continuous rock.

Walker? No, leaper. The three bounded exultant, little hindered by spacesuits, life support units, tool and ration packs. The naked land fled from their haste, and even higher, ever more clear and glorious to see, loomed the ice ahead of them.

There was no describing it, not really. You could speak of lower slopes and palisades above, to a mean height of perhaps a hundred meters, with spires towering farther still. You could speak of gracefully curved tiers going up those braes, of lacy parapets and fluted crags and arched openings to caves filled with wonders, of mysterious blues in the depths and greens where light streamed through translucencies, of gem-sparkle across whiteness where radiance and shadow wove mandalas—and none of it would convey anything more than Scobie's earlier, altogether inadequate comparison to the Grand Canyon.

"Stop," he said for the dozenth time. "I want to take a few pictures."

"Will anybody understand them who hasn't been here?" whispered Broberg.

"Probably not," said Garcilaso in the same hushed tone. "Maybe no one but us ever will."

"What do you mean by that?" demanded Danzig's voice.

"Never mind," snapped Scobie.

"I . . . think . . . I . . . know," the chemist said. "Yes, it is a great piece of scenery, but you're letting it hypnotize you."

"If you don't cut out that drivel," Scobie warned, "we'll cut you out of the circuit. Damn it, we've got work to do. Get off our backs."

Danzig gusted a sigh. "Sorry. Uh, are you finding any clues to the nature of that—that thing?"

Scobie focused his camera. "Well," he said, partly mollified, "the different shades and textures, and no doubt the different shapes, seem to confirm what the reflection spectra from the flyby suggested. The composition is a mixture, or a jumble, or both, of several materials, and varies from place to place. Water ice is obvious, but I feel sure of carbon dioxide too, and I'd bet on ammonia, methane, and presumably lesser amounts of other stuff."

"Methane? Could they stay solid at ambient temperature, in a vacuum?"

"We'll have to find out for sure. However, I'd guess that most of the time it's cold enough, at least for methane strata that occur down inside where there's pressure on them."

Within the vitryl globe of her helmet, Broberg's features showed delight. "Wait!" she cried. "I have an idea—about what happened to the probe that landed." She drew breath. "It came down almost at the foot of the glacier, you recall. Our view of the site from space seemed to indicate that an avalanche buried it, but we couldn't understand how that might have been triggered. Well, suppose a methane layer at exactly the wrong location melted. Heat radiation from the jets may have warmed it, and later the radar beam used to map contours added the last few degrees necessary. The stratum flowed, and down came everything that had rested on top of it."

"Plausible," Scobie said. "Congratulations, Jean."

"Nobody thought of the possibility in advance?" Garcilaso scoffed. "What kind of scientists have we got along?"

"The kind who were being overwhelmed by work after we reached Saturn, and still more by data input," Scobie answered. "The universe is bigger than you or anybody can realize, hotshot."

"Oh. Sure. No offense." Garcilaso's glance returned to the ice. "Yes, we'll never run out of mysteries, will we?"

"Never." Broberg's eyes glowed enormous. "At the heart of things will always be magic. The Elf King rules—"

Scobie returned his camera to its pouch. "Stow the gab and move on," he ordered curtly.

His gaze locked for an instant with Broberg's. In the weird, mingled light, it could be seen that she went pale, then red, before she sprang off beside him.

Ricia had gone alone into Moonwood on Midsummer Eve. The King found her there and took her unto him as she had hoped. Ecstasy became terror when he afterward bore her off; yet her captivity in the City of Ice brought her many more such hours, and beauties and marvels unknown among mortals. Alvarlan, her mentor, sent his spirit in quest of her, and was himself beguiled by what he found. It was an effort of will for him to tell Sir Kendrick of the Isles where she was, albeit he pledged his help in freeing her.

N'Kuma the Lionslayer, Béla of Eastmarch, Karina of the Far West, Lady Aurelia, Olav Harpmaster had none of them been present when this happened.

The glacier (a wrong name for something that might have no counterpart in the Solar System) lifted off the plain abruptly as a wall. Standing there, the three could no longer see the heights. They could, though, see that the slope which curved steeply upward to a filigree-topped edge was not smooth. Shadows lay blue in countless small craters. The sun had climbed just sufficiently high to beget them; a Iapetan day is more than seventy-nine of Earth's.

Danzig's question crackled in earphones:

"Now are you satisfied? Will you come back before a fresh landslide catches you?"

"It won't," Scobie replied. "We aren't a vehicle, and the local configuration has clearly been stable for centuries or better. Besides, what's the point of a manned expedition if nobody investigates anything?"

"I'll see if I can climb," Garcilaso offered.

"No, wait," Scobie commanded. "I've had experience with mountains and snowpacks, for whatever that may be worth. Let me study out a route for us first."

"You're going onto that stuff, the whole gaggle of you?" exploded Danzig. "Have you completely lost your minds?"

Scobie's brow and lips tightened. "Mark, I warn you again, if you don't get your emotions under control we'll cut you off. We'll hike on a ways if I decide it's safe."

He paced, in floating low-weight fashion, back and forth while he surveyed the jökull. Layers and blocks of distinct substances were plain to see, like separate ashlars laid by an elvish mason . . . where they were not so huge that a giant must have been at work . . . The craterlets might be sentry posts on this lowest embankment of the City's defenses. . . .

Garcilaso, most vivacious of men, stood motionless and let his vision lose itself in the sight. Broberg knelt down to examine the ground, but her own gaze kept wandering aloft.

Finally she beckoned. "Colin, come over here, please," she said. "I believe I've made a discovery."

Scobie joined her. As she rose, she scooped a

handful of fine black particles off the shards on which she stood and let it trickle from her glove. "I suspect this is the reason the boundary of the ice is sharp," she told him.

"What is?" Danzig inquired from afar. He got no answer.

"I noticed more and more dust as we went along," Broberg continued. "If it fell on patches and lumps of frozen stuff, isolated from the main mass, and covered them, it would absorb solar heat till they melted or, likelier, sublimed. Even water molecules would escape to space, in this weak gravity. The main mass was too big for that; square-cube law. Dust grains there would simply melt their way down a short distance, then be covered as surrounding material collapsed on them, and the process would stop."

"H'm." Broberg raised a hand to stroke his chin, encountered his helmet, and sketched a grin at himself. "Sounds reasonable. But where did so much dust come from—and the ice, for that matter?"

"I think—" Her voice dropped until he could barely hear, and her look went the way of Garcilaso's. His remained upon her face, profiled against stars. "I think this bears out your comet hypothesis, Colin. A comet struck Iapetus. It came from the direction it did because of getting so near Saturn that it was forced to swing in a hairpin bend around the planet. It was enormous; the ice of it covered almost a hemisphere, in spite of much more being vaporized and lost. The dust is partly from it, partly generated by the impact."

He clasped her armored shoulder. "*Your* theory, Jean. I was not the first to propose a comet, but you're the first to corroborate with details."

She didn't appear to notice, except that she murmured further: "Dust can account for the erosion that made those lovely formations, too. It caused differential melting and sublimation on the surface, according to the patterns it happened to fall in and the mixes of ices it clung to, until it was washed away or encysted. The craters, these small ones and the major ones we've observed from above, they have a separate but similar origin. Meteorites—"

"Whoa, there," he objected. "Any sizeable meteorite would release enough energy to steam off most of the entire field."

"I know. Which shows the comet collision was recent, less than a thousand yeas ago, or we wouldn't be seeing this miracle today. Nothing big has since happened to strike, yet. I'm thinking of little stones, cosmic sand, in prograde orbits around Saturn so that they hit with low relative speed. Most simply make dimples in the ice. Lying there, however, they collect solar heat because of being dark, and re-radiate it to melt away their surroundings, till they sink beneath. The concavities they leave reflect incident radiation from side to side, and thus continue to grow. The pothole effect. And again, because the different ices have different properties, you don't get perfectly smooth craters, but those fantastic bowls we saw before we landed."

"By God!" Scobie hugged her. "You're a genius."

Helmet against helmet, she smiled and said, "No. It's obvious, once you've seen for yourself." She was quiet for a bit while still they held each other. "Scientific intuition is a funny thing, I admit," she went on at last. "Considering the problem, I was hardly aware of my logical mind. What I thought was—the City of Ice, made with starstones out of that which a god called down from heaven—"

"Jesus Maria!" Garcilaso spun about to stare at them.

Scobie released the woman. "We'll go after confirmation," he said unsteadily. "To the large crater you'll remember we spotted a few klicks inward. The surface appears quite safe to walk on."

"I called that crater the Elf King's Dance Hall," Broberg mused, as if a dream were coming back to her.

"Have a care." Garcilaso's laugh rattled. "Heap big medicine yonder. The King is only an inheritor; it was giants who built these walls, for the gods."

"Well, I've got to find a way in, don't I?" Scobie responded.

"Indeed," *Alvarlan says.* "I cannot guide you from this point. My spirit can only see through mortal eyes. I can but lend you my counsel, until we have neared the gates."

"Are you sleepwalking in that fairytale of yours?" Danzig yelled. "Come back before you get yourselves killed!"

"Will you dry up?" Scobie snarled. "It's nothing but a style of talk we've got between us. If you can't understand that, you've got less use of your brain than we do."

"Listen, won't you? I didn't say you're crazy. You don't have delusions or anything like that. I do say you've steered your fantasies toward this kind of place, and now the reality has reinforced them till you're under a compulsion you don't recognize. Would you go ahead so recklessly anywhere else in the universe? Think!"

"That does it. We'll resume contact after you've had time to improve your manners." Scobie snapped off his main radio switch. The circuits that stayed active served for close-by communication but had no power to reach an orbital relay. His companions did likewise.

The three faced the awesomeness before them. "You can help me find the Princess when we are inside, Alvarlan," *Kendrick says.*

"That I can and will," *the sorcerer vows.*

"I wait for you, most steadfast of my lovers," *Ricia croons.*

Alone in the spacecraft, Danzig well-nigh sobbed, "Oh, damn that game forever!" The sound fell away into emptiness.

III

To condemn psychodrama, even in its enhanced form, would be to condemn human nature.

It begins in childhood. Play is necessary to an immature mammal, a means of learning to handle the body, the perceptions, and the outside world. The young human plays, must play, with its brain too. The more intelligent the child, the more its imagination needs exercise. There are degrees of activity, from the passive watching of a show on a screen, onward through reading, daydreaming, storytelling, and psychodrama . . . for which the child has no such fancy name.

We cannot give this behavior any single description, for the shape and course it takes depend on endlessly many variables. Sex, age, culture, and companions are only the most obvious. For example, in pre-electronic North America little girls would often play "house" while little boys played "cowboys and Indians" or "cops and robbers," whereas nowadays a mixed group of their descendants might play "dolphins" or "astronauts and aliens." In essence, a small band forms; each individual makes up a character to portray, or borrows one from fiction; simple props may be employed, such as toy weapons, or any chance object such as a stick may be declared something else such as a metal detector, or a thing may be quite imaginary, as the scenery almost always is. The children then act out a drama which they compose as they go along. When they cannot physically perform a certain action, they describe it. ("I jump real high, like you can do on Mars, an' come out over the edge o' that ol' Valles Marineris, an' take that bandit by surprise.") A large cast of characters, especially villains, frequently comes into existence by fiat.

The most imaginative member of the troupe dominates the game and the evolution of the story line, though in a rather subtle fashion, through offering the most vivid possibilities. The rest, however, are brighter than average; psychodrama in this highly developed form does not appeal to everybody.

For those to whom it does, the effects are beneficial and lifelong. Besides increasing their creativity through use, it lets them try out a play version of different adult roles and experiences. Thereby they begin to acquire insight into adulthood.

Such playacting ends when adolescence commences, if not earlier—but only in that form, and not necessarily forever in it. Grown-ups have many dream-games. This is plain to see in lodges, for example, with their titles, costumes, and ceremonies;

but does it not likewise animate all pageantry, every ritual? To what extent are our heroisms, sacrifices, and self-aggrandizements the acting out of personae that we maintain? Some thinkers have attempted to trace this element through very aspect of society.

Here, though, we are concerned with overt psychodrama among adults. In Western civilization it first appeared on a noticeable scale during the middle twentieth century. Psychiatrists found it a powerful diagnostic and therapeutic technique. Among ordinary folk, war and fantasy games, many of which involved identification with imaginary or historical characters, became increasingly popular. In part this was doubtless a retreat from the restrictions and menaces of that unhappy period, but likely in larger part it was a revolt of the mind against the inactive entertainment, notably television, which had come to dominate recreation.

The Chaos ended those activities. Everybody knows about their revival in recent times—for healthier reasons, one hopes. By projecting three-dimensional scenes and appropriate sounds from a data bank—or, better yet, by having a computer produce them to order—players gained a sense of reality that intensified their mental and emotional commitment. Yet in those games that went on for episode after episode, year after real-time year, whenever two or more members of a group could get together to play, they found themselves less and less dependent on such appurtenances. It seemed that, through practice, they had regained the vivid imaginations of their childhoods, and could make anything, or airy nothing itself, into the objects and the worlds they desired.

I have deemed it necessary thus to repeat the obvious in order that we may see it in perspective. The news beamed from Saturn has brought widespread revulsion. (Why? What buried fears have been touched? This is subject matter for potentially important research.) Overnight, adult psychodrama has become unpopular; it may become extinct. That would, in many ways, be a worse tragedy than what has occurred yonder. There is no reason to suppose that the game ever harmed any mentally sound person on Earth; on the contrary. Beyond doubt, it has helped astronauts stay sane and alert on long, difficult missions. If it has no more medical use, that is because psychotherapy has become a branch of applied biochemistry.

And this last fact, the modern world's dearth of experience with madness, is at the root of what happened. Although he could not have foreseen the exact outcome, a twentieth-century psychiatrist might have warned against spending eight years, an unprecedented stretch of time, in as strange an environment as the *Chronos*. Strange it certainly has been, despite all efforts—limited, totally man-controlled, devoid of countless cues for which our evolution on Earth has fashioned us. Extraterrestrial colonists have, thus far, had available to them any number of simulations and compensations, of which close, full contact with home and frequent opportunities to visit there are probably the most significant. Sailing time to Jupiter was long, but half of that to Saturn. Moreover, because they were earlier, scientists in the *Zeus* had much research to occupy them en route, which it would be pointless for later travelers to duplicate; by then, the interplanetary medium between the two giants held few surprises.

Contemporary psychologists were aware of this. They understood that the persons most adversely affected would be the most intelligent, imaginative, and dynamic—those who were supposed to make the very discoveries at Saturn which were the purpose of the undertaking. Being less familiar than their predecessors with the labyrinth that lies, Minotaur-haunted, beneath every human consciousness, the psychologists expected purely benign consequences of whatever psychodramas the crew engendered.

—Minamoto

Assignments to teams had not been made in advance of departure. It was sensible to let professional capabilities reveal themselves and grow on the voyage, while personal relationships did the same. Eventually such factors would help in deciding what individuals should train for what tasks. Long-term participation in a group of players normally forged bonds of friendship that were desirable, if the members were otherwise qualified.

In real life, Scobie always observed strict propriety toward Broberg. She was attractive, but she was monogamous, and he had no wish to alienate her. Besides, he liked her husband. (Tom did not partake of the game. As an astronomer, he had plenty to keep his attention happily engaged.) They had played for a couple of years, their bunch had acquired as many as it could accommodate in a narrative whose milieu and people were becoming complex, before Scobie and Broberg spoke of anything intimate.

By then, the story they enacted was doing so, and maybe it was not altogether by chance that they met when both had several idle hours. This was in the weightless recreation area at the spin axis. They tumbled through aerobatics, shouting and laughing, until they were pleasantly tired, went to the clubhouse, turned in their wingsuits, and showered. They had not seen each other nude before; neither commented, but he did not hide his enjoyment of the sight, while she colored and averted her glance as tactfully as she was able. Afterward, their clothes resumed, they decided on a drink before they went home, and sought the lounge.

Since evenwatch was approaching nightwatch, they had the place to themselves. At the bar, he thumbed a chit for Scotch, she for pinot chardonnay. The machine obliged them and they carried their refreshments out onto the balcony. Seated at a table, they looked across immensity. The clubhouse was built into the support frame on a Lunar gravity level. Above them they saw the sky wherein they had been as birds; its reach did not seem any more hemmed in by far-spaced, spidery girders than it was by a few drifting clouds. Beyond, and straight ahead, decks opposite were a commingling of masses and shapes which the scant illumination at this hour turned into mystery. Among those shadows the humans made out woods, brooks, pools, turned hoar or agleam by the light of stars which filled the skyview strips. Right and left, the hull stretched off beyond sight, a dark in which such lamps as there were appeared lost.

Air was cool, slightly jasmine-scented, drenched with silence. Underneath and throughout, subliminal, throbbed the myriad pulses of the ship.

"Magnificent," Broberg said low, gazing outward. "What a surprise."

"Eh?" asked Scobie.

"I've only been here before in daywatch. I didn't anticipate a simple rotation of the reflectors would make it wonderful."

"Oh, I wouldn't sneer at the daytime view. Mighty impressive."

"Yes, but—but then you see too plainly that everything is manmade, nothing is wild or unknown or free. The sun blots out the stars; it's as though no universe existed beyond this shell we're in. Tonight is like being in Maranoa," *the kingdom of which Ricia is Princess, a kingdom of ancient things and ways, wildernesses, enchantments.*

"H'm, yeah, sometimes I feel trapped myself," Scobie admitted. "I believed I had a journey's worth of geological data to study, but my project isn't going anywhere very interesting."

"Same for me." Broberg straightened where she sat, turned to him, and smiled a trifle. The dusk softened her features, made them look young. "Not that we're entitled to self-pity. Here we are, safe and comfortable till we reach Saturn. After that we should never lack for excitement, or for material to work with on the way home."

"True." Scobie raised his glass. "Well, skoal. Hope I'm not mispronouncing that."

"How should I know?" she laughed. "My maiden name was Almayer."

"That's right, you've adopted Tom's surname. I wasn't thinking. Though that is rather unusual these days, hey?"

She spread her hands. "My family was well-to-do, but they were—are—Jerusalem Catholics. Strict about certain things; archaistic, you might say." She lifted her wine and sipped. "Oh, yes, I've left the Church, but in several ways the Church will never leave me."

"I see. Not to pry, but, uh, this does account for some traits of yours I couldn't help wondering about."

She regarded him over the rim of her glass. "Like what?"

"Well, you've got a lot of life in you, vigor, sense of fun, but you're also—what's the word?—uncommonly domestic. You've told me you were a quiet faculty member of Yukon University till you married Tom." Scobie grinned. "Since you two kindly invited me to your last anniversary party, and I know your present age, I deduced that you were thirty then." Unmentioned was the likelihood that she had still been a virgin. "Nevertheless—oh, forget it. I said I don't want to pry."

"Go ahead, Colin," she urged. "That line from Burns sticks in my mind, since you introduced me to his poetry. 'To see oursels as others see us!' Since it looks as if we may visit the same moon—"

Scobie took a hefty dollop of Scotch. "Aw, nothing much," he said, unwontedly diffident. "If you must know, well, I have the impression that being in love wasn't the single good reason you had for marrying Tom. He'd already been accepted for this expedition, and given your personal qualifications, that would get you in too. In short, you'd grown tired of routine respectability and here was how you could kick over the traces. Am I right?"

"Yes." Her gaze dwelt on him. "You're more perceptive than I supposed."

"No, not really. A roughneck rockhound. But Ricia's made it plain to see, you're more than a demure wife, mother, and scientist—" She parted her lips. He raised a palm. "No, please, let me finish. I know it's bad manners to claim somebody's persona is a wish fulfillment, and I'm not doing that. Of course you don't want to be a free-roving, free-loving female scamp, any more than I want to ride around cutting down assorted enemies. Still, if you'd been born and raised in the world of our game, I feel sure you'd be a lot like Ricia. And that potential is part of you, Jean." He tossed off his drink. "If I've said too much, please excuse me. Want a refill?"

"I'd better not, but don't let me stop you."

"You won't." He rose and bounded off.

When he returned, he saw that she had been observing him through the vitryl door. As he sat down, she smiled, leaned a bit across the table, and told him softly: "I'm glad you said what you did. Now I can declare what a complicated man Kendrick reveals you to be."

"What?" Scobie asked in honest surprise. "Come on! He's a sword-and-shield tramp, a fellow who likes to travel, same as me; and in my teens I was a brawler, same as him."

"He may lack polish, but he's a chivalrous knight, a compassionate overlord, a knower of sagas and traditions, an appreciator of poetry and music, a bit of a bard . . . Ricia misses him. When will he get back from his latest quest?"

"I'm bound home this minute. N'Kuma and I gave those pirates the slip and landed at Haverness two days ago. After we buried the swag, he wanted to visit Béla and Karina and join them in whatever they've been up to, so we bade goodbye for the time being." Scobie and Harding had lately taken a few hours to conclude that adventure of theirs. The rest of the group had been mundanely occupied for some while.

Broberg's eyes widened. "From Haverness to the Isles? But I'm in Castle Devaranda, right in between."

"I hoped you'd be."

"I can't wait to hear your story."

"I'm pushing on after dark. The moon is bright and I've got a pair of remounts I bought with a few gold pieces from the loot." *The dust rolls white beneath drumming hoofs. Where a horseshoe strikes a flint pebble, sparks fly ardent. Kendrick scowls.* "You, aren't you, with . . . what's his name? . . . Joran the Red? I don't like him."

"I sent him packing a month ago. He got the

idea that sharing my bed gave him authority over me. It was never anything but a romp. I stand alone on the Gerfalcon Tower, looking south over moonlit fields, and wonder how you fare. The road flows toward me like a gray river. Do I see a rider come at a gallop, far and far away?"

After many months of play, no image on a screen was necessary. *Pennons on the night wind stream athwart the stars.* "I arrive. I sound my horn to rouse the gatekeepers."

"How I do remember those merry notes—"

That same night, Kendrick and Ricia become lovers. Experienced in the game and careful of its etiquette, Scobie and Broberg uttered no details about the union; they did not touch each other and maintained only fleeting eye contact; the ultimate goodnights were very decorous. After all, this was a story they composed about two fictitious characters in a world that never was.

The lower slopes of the jökull rose in tiers which were themselves deeply concave; the humans walked around their rims and admired the extravagant formations beneath. Names sprang onto lips, the Frost Garden, the Ghost Bridge, the Snow Queen's Throne, *while Kendrick advances into the City, and Ricia awaits him at the Dance Hall, and the spirit of Alvarlan carries word between them so that it is as if already she too travels beside her knight.* Nevertheless they proceeded warily, vigilant for signs of danger, especially whenever a change of texture or hue or anything else in the surface underfoot betokened a change in its nature.

Above the highest ledge reared a cliff too sheer to scale, Iapetan gravity or no, *the fortress wall*. However, from orbit the crew had spied a gouge in the vicinity, forming a pass, doubtless plowed by a small meteorite *in the war between the gods and the magicians, when stones chanted down from the sky wrought havoc so accursed that none dared afterward rebuild*. That was an eerie climb, hemmed in by heights which glimmered in the blue twilight they cast, heaven narrowed to a belt between them where stars seemed to blaze doubly brilliant.

"There must be guards at the opening," *Kendrick says*.

"A single guard," *answers the mind-whisper of Alvarlan*, "but he is a dragon. If you did battle with him, the noise and flame would bring every warrior here upon you. Fear not. I'll slip into his burnin' brain and weave him such a dream that he'll never see you."

"The King might sense the spell," *says Ricia through him*. "Since you'll be parted from us anyway while you ride the soul of that beast, Alvarlan, I'll seek him out and distract him."

Kendrick grimaces, knowing full well what means are hers to do that. She had told him how she longs for freedom and her knight; she has also hinted that elven lovemaking transcends the human. Does she wish for a final time before her rescue? . . . Well, Ricia and Kendrick have neither plighted nor practiced single troth. Assuredly Colin Scobie had not. He jerked forth a grin and continued through the silence that had fallen on all three.

They came out on top of the glacial mass and looked around them. Scobie whistled. Garcilaso stammered, "J-J-Jesus Christ!" Broberg smote her hands together.

Below them the precipice fell to the ledges, whose sculpturing took on a wholly new, eldritch aspect, gleam and shadow, until it ended at the plain. Seen from here aloft, the curvature of the moon made toes strain downward in boots, as if to cling fast and not be spun off among the stars which surrounded, rather than shone above, its ball. The spacecraft stood minute on dark, pocked stone, like a cenotaph raised to loneliness.

Eastward the ice reached beyond an edge of sight which was much closer. ("Yonder could be the rim of the world," Garcilaso said, and *Ricia replies,* "Yes, the City is nigh to there.") Bowls of different sizes, hillocks, crags, no two of them eroded the same way, turned its otherwise level stretch into a surreal maze. An arabesque openwork ridge which stood at the explorers' goal overtopped the horizon. Everything that was illuminated lay gently aglow. Radiant though the sun was, it cast the light of only, perhaps, five thousand full Lunas upon Earth. Southward, Saturn's great semidisc gave about one-half more Lunar shining; but in that direction, the wilderness sheened pale amber.

Scobie shook himself. "Well, shall we go?" His prosaic question jarred the others; Garcilaso frowned and Broberg winced.

She recovered. "Yes, hasten," *Ricia says.* "I am by myself once more. Are you out of the dragon's view, Alvarlan?"

"Ay," *the wizard informs her.* "Kendrick is safely behind a ruined palace. Tell us how best to reach you."

"You are at the time-gnawed Crown House. Before you lies the Street of the Shieldsmiths—"

Scobie's brows knitted. "It is noonday, when elves do not fare abroad," *Kendrick says* remindingly, commandingly. "I do not wish to encounter any of them. No fights, no complications. We are going to fetch you and escape, without further trouble."

Broberg and Garcilaso showed disappointment, but understood him. A game broke down when a person refused to accept something that a fellow player tried to put in. Often the narrative threads were not mended and picked up for many days. Broberg sighed.

"Follow the street to its end at a forum where a snow fountain springs,' *Ricia directs.* "Cross, and continue on Aleph Zain Boulevard. You will know it by a gateway in the form of a skull with open jaws. If anywhere you see a rainbow flicker in the air, stand motionless until it has gone by, for it will be an auroral wolf. . . ."

At a low-gravity lope, the distance took some thirty minutes to cover. In the later part, the three were forced to detour by great banks of an ice so fine-grained that it slid about under their bootsoles and tried to swallow them. Several of these lay at irregular intervals around their destination.

There the travelers stood again for a time in the grip of awe.

The bowl at their feet must reach down almost to bedrock, a hundred meters, and was twice as wide. On this rim lifted the wall they had seen from the cliff, an arc fifty meters long and high, nowhere thicker than five meters, pierced by intricate scrollwork, greenly agleam where it was not translucent. It was the uppermost edge of a stratum which made serrations down the crater. Other outcrops and ravines were more dreamlike yet . . . was that a unicorn's head, was that a colonnade of caryatids, was that an icicle bower. . . ? The depths were a lake of cold blue shadow.

"You have come, Kendrick, beloved!" *cries Ricia, and casts herself into his arms.*

"Quiet," *warns the sending of Alvarlan the wise.* "Rouse not our immortal enemies."

"Yes, we must get back." Scobie blinked. "Judas priest, what possessed us? Fun is fun, but we sure have come a lot farther and faster than was smart, haven't we?"

"Let us stay for a little while," Broberg pleaded. "This is such a miracle—the Elf King's Dance Hall, which the Lord of the Dance built for him—"

"Remember, if we stay we'll be caught, and your captivity may be forever." Scobie thumbed his main radio switch. "Hello, Mark? Do you read me?"

Neither Broberg nor Garcilaso made that move. They did not hear Danzig's voice: "Oh, yes! I've been hunkered over the set gnawing my knuckles. How are you?"

"All right. We're at the big hole and will be heading back as soon as I've gotten a few pictures."

"They haven't made words to tell how relieved I am. From a scientific standpoint, was it worth the risk?"

Scobie gasped. He stared before him.

"Colin?" Danzig called. "You still there?"

"Yes. Yes."

"I asked what observations of any importance you made."

"I don't know," Scobie mumbled. "I can't remember. None of it after we started climbing seems real."

"Better you return right away," Danzig said grimly. "Forget about photographs."

"Correct." Scobie addressed his companions: "Forward march."

"I can't," *Alvarlan answers*. "A wanderin' spell has caught my spirit in tendrils of smoke."

"I know where a fire dagger is kept," *Ricia says*. "I'll try to steal it."

Broberg moved ahead, as though to descend into the crater. Tiny ice grains trickled over the verge from beneath her boots. She could easily lose her footing and slide down.

"No, wait," *Kendrick shouts to her*. "No need. My spearhead is of moon alloy. It can cut—"

The glacier shuddered. The ridge cracked asunder and fell in shards. The area on which the humans stood split free and toppled into the bowl. An avalanche poured after. High-flung crystals caught sunlight, glittered prismatic in challenge to the stars, descended slowly and lay quiet.

Except for shock waves through solids, everything had happened in the absolute silence of space.

Heartbeat by heartbeat, Scobie crawled back to his senses. He found himself held down, immobilized, in darkness and pain. His armor had saved, was still saving his life; he had been stunned but escaped a real concussion. Yet every breath hurt abominably. A rib or two on the left side seemed broken; a monstrous impact must have dented metal. And he was buried under more weight than he could move.

"Hello," he coughed. "Does anybody read me?" The signal reply was the throb of his blood. If his radio still worked—which it should, being built into the suit—the mass around him screened him off.

It also sucked heat at an unknown but appalling rate. He felt no cold because the electrical system drew energy from his fuel cell as fast as needed to keep him warm and to recycle his air chemically. As a normal thing, when he lost heat through the slow process of radiation—and, a trifle, through kerofoam-lined bootsoles—the latter demand was much the greater. Now conduction was at work on every square centimeter. He had a spare unit in the equipment on his back, but no means of getting at it.

Unless— He barked forth a chuckle. Straining, he felt the stuff that entombed him yield the least bit under the pressure of arms and legs. And his helmet rang slightly with noise, a rustle, a gurgle. This wasn't water ice that imprisoned him, but stuff with a much lower freezing point. He was melting it, subliming it, making room for himself.

If he lay passive, he would sink, while frozenness above slid down to keep him in his grave. He might evoke superb new formations, but he would not see them. Instead, he must use the small capability given him to work his way upward, scrabble, get a purchase on matter that was not yet aflow, burrow to the stars.

He began.

Agony soon racked him, breath rasped in and out of lungs aflame, strength drained away and trembling took its place, he could not tell whether he ascended or slipped back. Blind, half suffocated, Scobie made mole-claws of his hands and dug.

It was too much to endure. He fled from it—

His strong enchantments failing, the Elf King brought down his towers of fear in wreck. If the spirit of Alvarlan returned to its body, the wizard would brood upon things he had seen, and understand what they meant, and such knowledge would give mortals a terrible power against Faerie. Waking from sleep, the King scryed Kendrick about to release that fetch. There was no time to do more than break the spell which upheld the Dance Hall. It was largely built of mist and starshine, but enough blocks quarried from the cold side of Ginnungagap were in it that when they crashed they should kill the knight. Ricia would perish too, and in his quicksilver intellect the King regret-

ted that. Nevertheless he spoke the necessary word.

He did not comprehend how much abuse flesh and bone can bear. Sir Kendrick fights his way clear of the ruins, to seek and save his lady. While he does, he heartens himself with thoughts of adventures past and future—

—and suddenly the blindness broke apart and Saturn stood lambent within rings.

Scobie belly-flopped onto the surface and lay shuddering.

He must rise, no matter how his injuries screamed, lest he melt himself a new burial place. He lurched to his feet and glared around.

Little but outcroppings and scars was left of the sculpture. For the most part, the crater had become a smooth-sided whiteness under heaven. Scarcity of shadows made distances hard to gauge, but Scobie guessed the new depth as about seventy-five meters. And empty, empty.

"Mark, do you hear?" he cried.

"That you, Colin?" rang in his earpieces. "Name of mercy, what's happened? I heard you call out, and saw a cloud rise and sink . . . then nothing for more than an hour. Are you okay?"

"I am, sort of. I don't see Jean or Luis. A landslide took us by surprise and buried us. Hold on while I search."

When he stood upright, Scobie's ribs hurt less. He could move about rather handily if he took care. The two types of standard analgesic in his kit were alike useless, one too weak to give noticeable relief, one so strong that it would turn him sluggish. Casting to and fro, he soon found what he expected, a concavity in the tumbled snowlike material, slightly aboil.

Also a standard part of his gear was a trenching tool. Scobie set pain aside and dug. A helmet appeared. Broberg's head was within it. She too had been tunneling out.

"Jean!"—"Kendrick!" She crept free and they embraced, suit to suit. "Oh, Colin."

"How are you?" rattled from him.

"Alive," she answered. "No serious harm done, I think. A lot to be said for low gravity. . . . You? Luis?" Blood was clotted in a streak beneath her nose, and a bruise on her forehead was turning purple, but she stood firmly and spoke clearly.

"I'm functional. Haven't found Luis yet. Help me look. First, though, we'd better check out our equipment."

She hugged arms around chest, as if that would do any good here. "I'm chilled," she admitted.

Scobie pointed at a telltale. "No wonder. Your fuel cell's down to its last couple of ergs. Mine isn't in a lot better shape. Let's change."

They didn't waste time removing their backpacks, but reached into each other's. Tossing the spent units to the ground, where vapors and holes immediately appeared and then froze, they plugged the fresh ones into their suits. "Turn your thermostat down," Scobie advised. "We won't find shelter soon. Physical activity will help us keep warm."

"And require faster air recycling," Broberg reminded.

"Yeah. But for the moment, at least, we can

conserve the energy in the cells. Okay, next let's check for strains, potential leaks, any kind of damage or loss. Hurry. Luis is still down underneath."

Inspection was a routine made automatic by years of drill. While her fingers searched across the man's spacesuit, Broberg let her eyes wander. "The Dance Hall is gone," *Ricia murmurs.* "I think the King smashed it to prevent our escape."

"Me too. If he finds out we're alive, and seeking for Alvarlan's soul—Hey, wait! None of that!"

Danzig's voice quavered. "How're you doing?"

"We're in fair shape, seems like," Scobie replied. "My corselet took a beating but didn't split or anything. Now to find Luis . . . Jean, suppose you spiral right, I left, across the crater floor."

It took a while, for the seething which marked Garcilaso's burial was minuscule. Scobie started to dig. Broberg watched how he moved, heard how he breathed, and said, "Give me that tool. Just where are you bunged up, anyway?"

He admitted his condition and stepped back. Crusty chunks flew from her toil. She progressed fast, since whatever kind of ice lay at this point was, luckily, friable, and under Iapetan gravity she could cut a hole with almost vertical sides.

"I'll make myself useful," Scobie said, "namely, find us a way out."

When he started up the nearest slope, it shivered. All at once he was borne back in a tide that made rustly noises through his armor, while a fog of dry white motes blinded him. Painfully, he scratched himself free at the bottom and tried elsewhere. In the end he could report to Danzig: "I'm afraid there is no easy route. When the rim collapsed where we stood, it did more than produce a shock which wrecked the delicate formations throughout the crater. It let tons of stuff pour down from the surface—a particular sort of ice that, under local conditions, is like fine sand. The walls are covered by it. Most places, it lies meters deep over more stable material. We'd slide faster than we could climb, where the layer is thin; where it's thick, we'd sink."

Danzig sighed. "I guess I get to take a nice, healthy hike."

"I assume you've called for help."

"Of course. They'll have two boats here in about a hundred hours. The best they can manage. You knew that already."

"Uh-huh. And our fuel cells are good for perhaps fifty hours."

"Oh, well, not to worry about that. I'll bring extras and toss them to you, if you're stuck till the rescue party arrives. M-m-m . . . maybe I'd better rig a slingshot or something first."

"You might have a problem locating us. This isn't a true crater, it's a glorified pothole, the lip of it flush with the top of the glacier. The landmark we guided ourselves by, that fancy ridge, is gone."

"No big deal. I've got a bearing on you from the directional antenna, remember. A magnetic compass may be of no use here, but I can keep myself oriented by the heavens. Saturn scarcely moves in this sky, and the sun and the stars don't move fast."

"Damn! You're right. I wasn't thinking. Got Luis on my mind, if nothing else." Scobie looked across bleakness toward Broberg. Perforce she was taking a short rest, stoop-shouldered above her excavation. His earpieces brought him the harsh sound in her windpipe.

He must maintain what strength was left him, against later need. He sipped from his water nipple, pushed a bite of food through his chowlock, pretended an appetite. "I may as well try reconstructing what happened," he said. "Okay, Mark, you were right, we got crazy reckless. The game—Eight years was too long to play the game, in an environment that gave us too few reminders of reality. But who could have foreseen it? My God, warn *Chronos*! I happen to know that one of the Titan teams started playing an expedition to the merfolk under the Crimson Ocean—on account of the red mists—deliberately, like us, before they set off. . . ."

Scobie gulped. "Well," he slogged on, "I don't suppose we'll ever know exactly what went wrong here. But plain to see, the configuration was only metastable. On Earth, too, avalanches can be fatally easy to touch off. I'd guess at a methane layer underneath the surface. It turned a little slushy when temperatures rose after dawn, but that didn't matter in low gravity and vacuum . . . till we came along. Heat, vibration—Anyhow, the stratum slid out from under us, which triggered a general collapse. Does that guess seem reasonable?"

"Yes, to an amateur like me," Danzig said. "I admire how you can stay academic under these circumstances."

"I'm being practical," Scobie retorted. "Luis may need medical attention earlier than those boats can come for him. If so, how do we get him to ours?"

Danzig's voice turned stark. "Any ideas?"

"I'm fumbling my way toward that. Look, the bowl still has the same basic form. The whole shebang didn't cave in. That implies hard material, water ice and actual rock. In fact, I see a few remaining promontories, jutting out above the sandlike stuff. As for what *it* is—maybe an ammonia-carbon dioxide combination, maybe more exotic—that'll be for you to discover later. Right now . . . my geological instruments should help me trace where the solid masses are least deeply covered. We all carry trenching tools, of course. We can try to shovel a path clear, along a zigzag of least effort. Sure, that may well often bring more garbage slipping down on us from above, but that in turn may expedite our progress. Where the uncovered shelves are too steep or slippery to climb, we can chip footholds. Slow and tough work; and we may run into a bluff higher than we can jump, or something like that."

"I can help," Danzig proposed. "While I waited to hear from you, I inventoried our stock of spare cable, cord, equipment I can cannibalize for wire, clothes and bedding I can cut into strips, whatever might be knotted together to make a rope. We won't need much tensile strength. Well, I estimate I can get about forty meters. According to your description, that's about half the slope length of that trap you're in. If you can climb halfway up while I trek there, I can haul you the rest of the way."

"Thanks," Scobie said, "although—"

"Luis!" shrieked in his helmet. "Colin, come fast, help me, this is dreadful!"

Regardless of pain, except for a curse or two, Scobie sped to Broberg's aid.

Garcilaso was not quite unconscious. In that lay much of the horror. They heard him mumble, "—Hell, the King threw my soul into Hell, I can't find my way out, I'm lost, if only Hell weren't so cold—" They could not see his face; the inside of his helmet was crusted with frost. Deeper and longer buried than the others, badly hurt in addition, he would have died shortly after his fuel cell was exhausted. Broberg had uncovered him barely in time, if that.

Crouched in the shaft she had dug, she rolled him over onto his belly. His limbs flopped about and he babbled, "A demon attacks me, I'm blind here but I feel the wind of its wings," in a blurred monotone. She unplugged the energy unit and tossed it aloft, saying, "We should return this to the ship if we can." Not uncommonly do trivial details serve as crutches.

Above, Scobie gave the object a morbid stare. It didn't even retain the warmth to make a little vapor, like his and hers, but lay quite inert. Its case was a metal box, thirty centimeters by fifteen by six, featureless except for two plug-in prongs on one of the broad sides. Controls built into the spacesuit circuits allowed you to start and stop the chemical reactions within and regulate their rate manually; but as a rule you left that chore to your thermostat and aerostat. Now those reactions had run their course. Until it was recharged, the cell was merely a lump.

Scobie leaned over to watch Broberg, some ten meters below him. She had extracted the reserve unit from Garcilaso's gear, inserted it properly at the small of his back, and secured it by clips on the bottom of his packframe. "Let's have your contribution, Colin," she said. Scobie dropped the meter of heavy-gauge insulated wire which was standard issue on extravehicular missions, in case you needed to make a special electrical connection or a repair. She joined it by Western Union splices to the two she already had, made a loop at the end and, awkwardly reaching over her left shoulder, secured the opposite end by a hitch to the top of her packframe. The triple strand bobbled above her like an antenna.

Stooping, she gathered Garcilaso in her arms. The Iapetan weight of him and his apparatus was under ten kilos, of her and hers about the same. Theoretically she could jump straight out of the hole with her burden. In practice, her spacesuit was too hampering; constant-volume joints allowed considerable freedom of movement, but not as much as bare skin, especially when circum-Saturnian temperatures required extra insulation. Besides, if she could have reached the top, she could not have stayed. Soft ice would have crumbled beneath her fingers and she would have tumbled back down.

"Here goes," she said. "This had better be right the first time, Colin. I don't think Luis can take much jouncing."

"Kendrick, Ricia, where are you?" Garcilaso moaned. "Are you in Hell too?"

Scobie dug heels into the ground near the edge and crouched ready. The loop in the wire rose to view. His right hand grabbed hold. He threw himself backward, lest he slide forward, and felt the mass he had captured slam to a halt. Anguish exploded in his rib cage. Somehow he dragged his burden to safety before he fainted.

He came out of that in a minute. "I'm okay," he rasped at the anxious voices of Broberg and Danzig. "Only lemme rest a while."

The physicist nodded and knelt to minister to the pilot. She stripped his packframe in order that he might lie flat on it, head and legs supported by the packs themselves. That would prevent significant heat loss by convection and cut loss by conduction. Still, his fuel cell would be drained faster than if he were on his feet, and first it had a terrible energy deficit to make up.

"The ice is clearing away inside his helmet," she reported. "Merciful Mary, the blood! Seems to be from the scalp, though; it isn't running any more. His occiput must have been slammed against the vitryl. We ought to wear padded caps in these rigs. Yes, I know accidents like this haven't happened before, but—" She unclipped the flashlight at her waist, stooped, and shone it downward. "His eyes are open. The pupils—yes, a severe concussion, and likely a skull fracture, which may be hemorrhaging into the brain. I'm surprised he isn't vomiting. Did the cold prevent that? Will he start soon? He could choke on his own vomit, in there where nobody can lay a hand on him."

Scobie's pain had subsided to a bearable intensity. He rose, went over to look, whistled, and said, "I judge he's doomed unless we get him to the boat and give him proper care almighty soon. Which isn't possible."

"Oh, Luis." Tears ran silently down Broberg's cheeks.

"You think he can't last till I bring my rope and we carry him back?" Danzig asked.

" 'Fraid not," Scobie replied. "I've taken paramedical courses, and in fact I've seen a case like this before. How come you know the symptoms, Jean?"

"I read a lot," she said dully.

"They weep, the dead children weep," Garcilaso muttered.

Danzig sighed. "Okay, then. I'll fly over to you."

"*Huh?*" burst from Scobie, and from Broberg: "Have you also gone insane?"

"No, listen," Danzig said fast. "I'm no skilled pilot, but I have the same basic training in this type of craft that everybody does who might ride in one. It's expendable; the rescue vessels can bring us back. There'd be no significant gain if I landed close to the glacier—I'd still have to make that rope and so forth—and we know from what happened to the probe that there would be a real hazard. Better I make straight for your crater."

"Coming down on a surface that the jets will vaporize out from under you?" Scobie snorted. "I bet Luis would consider that a hairy stunt. You, my friend, would crack up."

"Nu?" They could almost see the shrug. "A crash from low altitude, in this gravity, shouldn't do more than rattle my teeth. The blast will cut a hole clear to bedrock. True, then surrounding ice will collapse in around the hull and trap it. You may need to dig to reach the airlock, though I suspect thermal radiation from the cabin will keep the upper parts of the structure free. Even if the craft topples and strikes sidewise—in which case, it'll sink down into a deflating cushion—even if it did that on bare rock, it shouldn't be seriously damaged. It's designed to withstand heavier impacts." Danzig hesitated. "Of course, could be this would endanger you. I'm confident I won't fry you with the jets, assuming I descend near the middle and you're as far offside as you can get. Maybe, though, maybe I'd cause a . . . an ice quake that'll kill you. No sense in losing two more lives."

"Or three, Mark," Broberg said low. "In spite of your brave words, you could come to grief yourself."

"Oh, well, I'm an oldish man. I'm fond of living, yes, but you guys have a whole lot more years due you. Look, suppose the worst, suppose I don't just make a messy landing but wreck the boat utterly. Then Luis dies, but he would anyway. You two, however, you should have access to the stores aboard, including those extra fuel cells. I'm willing to run what I consider to be a small risk of my own neck, for the sake of giving Luis a chance at survival."

"Um-m-m," went Scobie, deep in his throat. A hand strayed in search of his chin, while his gaze roved around the glimmer of the bowl.

"I repeat," Danzig proceeded, "if you think this might jeopardize you in any way, we scrub it. No heroics, please. Luis would surely agree, better three people safe and one dead than four stuck with a high probability of death."

"Let me think." Scobie was mute for minutes before he said: "No, I don't believe we'd get in too much trouble here. As I remarked earlier, the vicinity has had its avalanche and must be in a reasonably stable configuration. True, ice will volatilize. In the case of deposits with low boiling points, that could happen explosively and cause tremors. But the vapor will carry heat away so fast that only material in your immediate area should change state. I daresay that the fine-grained stuff will get shaken down the slopes, but it's got too low a density to do serious harm; for the most part, it should simply act like a brief snowstorm. The floor will make adjustments, of course, which may be rather violent. However, we can be above it—do you see that shelf of rock over yonder, Jean, at jumping height? It has to be part of a buried hill; solid. That's our place to wait. . . . Okay,

Mark, it's go as far as we're concerned. I can't be absolutely certain, but who ever is about anything? It seems like a good bet."

"What are we overlooking?" Broberg wondered. She glanced down to him who lay at her feet. "While we considered all the possibilities, Luis would die. Yes, fly if you want to, Mark, and God bless you."

—But when she and Scobie had brought Garcilaso to the ledge, she gestured from Saturn to Polaris and: "I will sing a spell, I will cast what small magic is mine, in aid of the Dragon Lord, that he may deliver Alvarlan's soul from Hell," *says Ricia.*

IV

No reasonable person will blame any interplanetary explorer for miscalculations about the actual environment, especially when *some* decision has to be made, in haste under stress. Occasional errors are inevitable. If we knew exactly what to expect throughout the Solar System, we would have no reason to explore it.

—Minamoto

The boat lifted. Cosmic dust smoked away from its jets. A hundred and fifty meters aloft, thrust lessened and it stood still on a pillar of fire.

Within the cabin was little noise, a low hiss and a bone-deep but nearly inaudible rumble. Sweat studded Danzig's features, clung glistening to his beard stubble, soaked his coverall and made it reek. He was about to undertake a maneuver as difficult as rendezvous, and without guidance.

Gingerly, he advanced a vernier. A side jet woke. The boat lurched toward a nosedive. Danzig's hands jerked across the console. He must adjust the forces that held his vessel on high and those that pushed it horizontally, to get a resultant that would carry him eastward at a slow, steady pace. The vectors would change instant by instant, as they do when a human walks. The control computer, linked to the sensors, handled much of the balancing act, but not the crucial part. He must tell it what he wanted it to do.

His handling was inexpert. He had realized it would be. More altitude would have given him more margin for error, but deprived him of cues that his eyes found on the terrain beneath and the horizon ahead. Besides, when he reached the glacier he would perforce fly low, to find his goal. He would be too busy for the precise celestial navigation he could have practiced afoot.

Seeking to correct his error, he overcompensated, and the boat pitched in a different direction. He punched for "hold steady" and the computer took over. Motionless again, he took a minute to catch his breath, regain his nerve, rehearse in his mind. Biting his lip, he tried afresh. This time he did not quite approach disaster. Jets aflicker, the boat staggered drunkenly over the moonscape.

The ice cliff loomed nearer and nearer. He

saw its fragile loveliness and regretted that he must cut a swathe of ruin. Yet what did any natural wonder mean unless a conscious mind was there to know it? He passed the lowest slope. It vanished in billows of steam.

Onward. Beyond the boiling, right and left and ahead, the Faerie architecture crumbled. He crossed the palisade. Now he was a bare fifty meters above surface, and the clouds reached vengefully close before they disappeared into vacuum. He squinted through the port and made the scanner sweep a magnified overview across its screen, a search for his destination.

A white volcano erupted. The outburst engulfed him. Suddenly he was flying blind. Shocks belled through the hull when upflung stones hit. Frost sheathed the craft; the scanner screen went as blank as the ports. Danzig should have ordered ascent, but he was inexperienced. A human in danger has less of an instinct to jump than to run. He tried to scuttle sideways. Without exterior vision to aid him, he sent the vessel tumbling end over end. By the time he saw his mistake, less than a second, it was too late. He was out of control. The computer might have retrieved the situation after a while, but the glacier was too close. The boat crashed.

"Hello, Mark?" Scobie cried. "Mark, do you read me? Where are you, for Christ's sake?"

Silence replied. He gave Broberg a look which lingered. "Everything seemed to be in order," he said, "till we heard a shout, and a lot of racket, and nothing. He should've reached us by now. Instead, he's run into trouble. I hope it wasn't lethal."

"What can we do?" she asked as redundantly. They needed talk, any talk, for Garcilaso lay beside them and his delirious voice was dwindling fast.

"If we don't get fresh fuel cells within the next forty or fifty hours, we'll be at the end of our particular trail. The boat should be someplace near. We'll have to get out of this hole under our own power, seems like. Wait here with Luis and I'll scratch around for a possible route."

Scobie started downward. Broberg crouched by the pilot.

"—alone forever in the dark—" she heard.

"No, Alvarlan." She embraced him. Most likely he could not feel that, but she could. "Alvarlan, hearken to me. This is Ricia. I hear in my mind how your spirit calls. Let me help, let me lead you back to the light."

"Have a care," advised Scobie. "We're too damn close to rehypnotizing ourselves as is."

"But I might, I just might get through to Luis and . . . comfort him . . . Alvarlan, Kendrick and I escaped. He's seeking a way home for us. I'm seeking you. Alvarlan, here is my hand, come take it."

On the crater floor, Scobie shook his head, clicked his tongue, and unlimbered his equipment. Binoculars would help him locate the most promising areas. Devices that ranged from a metal rod to a portable geosonar would give him a more exact idea of what sort of footing lay buried under what depth of unclimbable sand-ice. Admittedly the scope of such probes was very limited. He did not have time to shovel tons of material aside in order that he could mount higher and test further. He would simply have to get some preliminary results, make an educated guess at which path up the side of the bowl would prove negotiable, and trust he was right.

He shut Broberg and Garcilaso out of his consciousness as much as he was able, and commenced work.

An hour later, he was ignoring pain while clearing a strip across a layer of rock. He thought a berg of good, hard frozen water lay ahead, but wanted to make sure.

"Jean! Colin! Do you read?"

Scobie straightened and stood rigid. Dimly he heard Broberg: "If I can't do anything else, Alvarlan, let me pray for your soul's repose."

"Mark!" ripped from Scobie. "You okay? What the hell happened?"

"Yeah, I wasn't too badly knocked around," Danzig said, "and the boat's habitable, though I'm afraid it'll never fly again. How are you? Luis?"

"Sinking fast. All right, let's hear the news."

Danzig described his misfortune. "I wobbled off in an unknown direction for an unknown distance. It can't have been extremely far, since the time was short before I hit. Evidently I plowed into a large, um, snowbank, which softened the impact but blocked radio transmission. It's evaporated from the cabin area now. I see tumbled whiteness around, and formations in the offing. . . . I'm not sure what damage the jacks and the stern jets suffered. The boat's on its side at about a forty-five degree angle, presumably with rock beneath. But the after part is still buried in less whiffable stuff—water and CO_2 ices, I think—that's reached temperature equilibrium. The jets must be clogged with it. If I tried to blast, I'd destroy the whole works."

Scobie nodded. "You would, for sure."

Danzig's voice broke. "Oh, God, Colin! What have I done? I wanted to help Luis, but I may have killed you and Jean."

Scobie's lips tightened. "Let's not start crying before we're hurt. True, this has been quite a run of bad luck. But neither you nor I nor anybody could have known that you'd touch off a bomb underneath yourself."

"What was it? Have you any notion? Nothing of the sort ever occurred at rendezvous with a comet. And you believe the glacier is a wrecked comet, don't you?"

"Uh-huh, except that conditions have obviously modified it. The impact produced heat, shock, turbulence. Molecules got scrambled. Plasmas must have been momentarily present. Mixtures, compounds, clathrates, alloys—stuff formed that never existed in free space. We can learn a lot of chemistry here."

"That's why I came along. . . . Well, then, I crossed a deposit of some substance or substances that the jets caused to sublime with tremendous force. A certain kind of vapor refroze when it encountered the hull. I had to defrost the ports from inside after the snow had cooked off them."

"Where are you in relation to us?"

"I told you, I don't know. And I'm not sure I can determine it. The crash crumpled the direction-finding antenna. Let me go outside for a better look."

"Do that," Scobie said. "I'll keep busy meanwhile."

He did, until a ghastly rattling noise and Broberg's wail brought him at full speed back to the rock.

Scobie switched off Garcilaso's fuel cell. "This may make the difference that carries us through," he said low. "Think of it as a gift. Thanks, Luis."

Broberg let go of the pilot and rose from her knees. She straightened the limbs that had threshed about in the death struggle and crossed his hands on his breast. There was nothing she could do about the fallen jaw or the eyes that glared at heaven. Taking him out of his suit, here, would have worsened his appearance. Nor could she wipe tears off her own face. She could merely try to stop their flow. "Goodbye, Luis," she whispered.

Turning to Scobie, she asked, "Can you give me a new job? Please."

"Come along," he directed. "I'll explain what I have in mind about making our way to the surface."

They were midway across the bowl when Danzig called. He had not let his comrade's dying slow his efforts, nor said much while it happened. Once, most softly, he had offered Kaddish.

"No luck," he reported like a machine. "I've traversed the largest circle I could while keeping the boat in sight, and found only weird, frozen shapes. I can't be a huge distance from you, or I'd see an identifiably different sky, on this miserable little ball. You're probably within a twenty or thirty kilometer radius of me. But that covers a bunch of territory."

"Right," Scobie said. "Chances are you can't find us in the time we've got. Return to the boat."

"Hey, wait," Danzig protested. "I can spiral onward, marking my trail. I might come across you."

"It'll be more useful if you return," Scobie told him. "Assuming we climb out, we should be able to hike to you, but we'll need a beacon. What occurs to me is the ice itself. A small energy release, if it's concentrated, should release a large plume of methane or something similarly volatile. The gas will cool as it expands, recondense around dust particles that have been carried along—it'll steam—and the cloud ought to get high enough, before it evaporates again, to be visible from here."

"Gotcha!" A tinge of excitement livened Danzig's words. "I'll go straight to it. Make tests, find a spot where I can get the showiest result, and . . . how about I rig a thermite bomb? . . . No, that might be too hot. Well, I'll develop a gadget."

"Keep us posted."

"But I, I don't think we'll care to chatter idly," Broberg ventured.

"No, we'll be working our tails off, you and I," Scobie agreed.

"Uh, wait," said Danzig. "What if you find you can't get clear to the top? You implied that's a distinct possibility."

"Well, then it'll be time for more radical procedures, whatever they turn out to be," Scobie responded. "Frankly, at this moment my head is too full of . . . of Luis, and of choosing an optimum escape route . . . for much thought about anything else."

"M-m, yeah, I guess we've got an ample supply of trouble without borrowing more. Tell you what, though. After my beacon's ready to fire off, I'll make that rope we talked of. You might find you prefer having it to clean clothes and sheets when you arrive." Danzig was silent for seconds before he ended: "God damn it, you *will* arrive."

Scobie chose a point on the north side for his and Broberg's attempt. Two rock shelves jutted forth, near the floor and several meters higher, indicating that stone reached at least that far. Beyond, in a staggered pattern, were similar outcrops of hard ices. Between them, and onward from the uppermost, which was scarcely more than halfway to the rim, was nothing but the featureless, footingless slope of powder crystals. Its angle of repose gave a steepness that made the surface doubly treacherous. The question, unanswerable save by experience, was how deeply it covered layers on which humans could climb, and whether such layers extended the entire distance aloft.

At the spot, Scobie signalled a halt. "Take it easy, Jean," he said. "I'll go ahead and commence digging."

"Why don't we together? I have my own tool, you know."

"Because I can't tell how so large a bank of that pseudo-quicksand will behave. It might react to the disturbance by a gigantic slide."

She bridled. Her haggard countenance registered mutiny. "Why not me first, then? Do you suppose I always wait passive for Kendrick to save me?"

"As a matter of fact," he rapped, "I'll bargain because my rib is giving me billy hell, which is eating away what strength I've got left. If we run into trouble, you can better come to my help than I to yours."

Broberg bent her neck. "Oh. I'm sorry. I must be in a fairly bad state myself, if I let false pride interfere with our business." Her look went toward Saturn, around which *Chronos* orbited, bearing her husband and children.

"You're forgiven." Scobie bunched his legs and sprang the five meters to the lower ledge. The next one was slightly too far for such a jump, when he had no room for a running start.

Stooping, he scraped his trenching tool against the bottom of the declivity that sparkled before him, and shoveled. Grains poured from above, a billionfold, to cover what he cleared. He worked like a robot possessed. Each spadeful was nearly weightless, but the number of spadefuls was nearly endless. He did not bring the entire bowlside down on himself as he had half feared, half hoped. (If that didn't kill him, it would save a lot of toil.) A dry torrent went right and left over his ankles. Yet at last somewhat more of the underlying rock began to show.

From beneath, Broberg listened to him breathe. It sounded rough, often broken by a gasp or a curse. In his spacesuit, in the raw, wan sunshine, he resembled a knight who, in despite of wounds, did battle against a monster.

"All right," he called at last. "I think I've learned what to expect and how we should operate. It'll take the two of us."

"Yes . . . oh, yes, my Kendrick."

The hours passed. Ever so slowly, the sun climbed and the stars wheeled and Saturn waned.

Most places, the humans labored side by side. They did not require more than the narrowest of lanes—but unless they cut it wide to begin with, the banks to right and left would promptly slip down and bury it. Sometimes the conformation underneath allowed a single person at a time to work. Then the other could rest. Soon it was Scobie who must oftenest take advantage of that. Sometimes they both stopped briefly, for food and drink and reclining on their packs.

Rock yielded to water ice. Where this rose very sharply, the couple knew it, because the sand-ice that they undercut would come down in a mass. After the first such incident, when they were nearly swept away, Scobie always drove his geologist's hammer into each new stratum. At any sign of danger, he would seize its handle and Broberg would cast an arm around his waist. Their other hands clutched their trenching tools, Anchored, but forced to strain every muscle, they would stand while the flood poured around them, knee-high, once even chest-high, seeking to bury them irretrievably deep in its quasi-fluid substance. Afterward they would confront a bare stretch. It was generally too steep to climb unaided, and they chipped footholds.

Weariness was another tide to which they dared not yield. At best, their progress was dismayingly slow. They needed little heat input to keep warm, except when they took a rest, but their lungs put a furious demand on air recyclers. Garcilaso's fuel cell, which they had brought along, could give a single person extra hours of life, though depleted as it was after coping with his hypothermia, the time would be insufficient for rescue by the teams from *Chronos*. Unspoken was the idea of taking turns with it. That would put them in wretched shape, chilled and stifling, but at least they would leave the universe together.

Thus it was hardly a surprise that their minds fled from pain, soreness, exhaustion, stench, despair. Without that respite, they could not have gone on as long as they did.

At ease for a few minutes, their backs against a blue-shimmering parapet which they must scale, they gazed across the bowl, where Garcilaso's suited body gleamed like a remote pyre, and up the curve opposite to Saturn. The planet shone lambent amber, softly banded, the rings a coronet which a shadow band across their arc seemed to make all the brighter. That radiance overcame sight of most nearby stars, but elsewhere they arrayed themselves multitudinous, in splendor, around the silver road which the galaxy clove between them.

"How right a tomb for Alvarlan," *Ricia says in a dreamer's murmur.*

"Has he died, then?" *Kendrick asks.*

"You do not know?"

"I have been too busied. After we won free of the ruins and I left you to recover while I went scouting, I encountered a troop of warriors. I escaped, but must needs return to you by devious, hidden ways." *Kendrick strokes Ricia's sunny hair.* "Besides, dearest dear, it has ever been you, not I, who had the gift of hearing spirits."

"Brave darling. . . . Yes, it is a glory to me that I was able to call his soul out of Hell. It sought his body, but that was old and frail and could not survive the knowledge it now had. Yet Alvarlan passed peacefully, and before he did, for his last magic he made himself a tomb from whose ceiling starlight will eternally shine."

"May he sleep well. But for us there is no sleep. Not yet. We have far to travel."

"Aye. But already we have left the wreckage behind. Look! Everywhere around in this meadow, anemones peep through the grass. A lark sings above."

"These lands are not always calm. We may

well have more adventures ahead of us. But we shall meet them with high hearts."

Kendrick and Ricia rise to continue their journey.

Cramped on a meager ledge, Scobie and Broberg shoveled for an hour without broadening it much. The sand-ice slid from above as fast as they could cast it down. "We'd better quit this as a bad job," the man finally decided. "The best we've done is flatten the slope ahead of us a tiny bit. No telling how far inward the shelf goes before there's a solid layer on top. Maybe there isn't any."

"What shall we do instead?" Broberg asked in the same worn tone.

He jerked a thumb. "Scramble back to the level beneath and try a different direction. But first we absolutely require a break."

They spread kerofoam pads and sat. After a while during which they merely stared, stunned by fatigue, Broberg spoke.

"I go to the brook," *Ricia relates.* "It chimes under arches of green boughs. Light falls between them to sparkle on it. I kneel and drink. The water is cold, pure, sweet. When I raise my eyes, I see the figure of a young woman, naked, her tresses the color of leaves. A wood nymph. She smiles."

"Yes, I see her too," *Kendrick joins in.* "I approach carefully, not to frighten her off. She asks our names and errands. We explain that we are lost. She tells us how to find an oracle which may give us counsel."

They depart to find it.

* * *

Flesh could no longer stave off sleep. "Give us a yell in an hour, will you, Mark?" Scobie requested.

"Sure," Danzig said, "but will that be enough?"

"It's the most we can afford, after the setbacks we've had. We've come less than a third of the way."

"If I haven't talked to you," Danzig said slowly, "it's not because I've been hard at work, though I have been. It's that I figured you two were having a plenty bad time without me nagging you. However—Do you think it's wise to fantasize the way you have been?"

A flush crept across Broberg's cheeks and down toward her bosom. "You listened, Mark?"

"Well, yes, of course. You might have an urgent word for me at any minute—"

"Why? What could you do? A game is a personal affair."

"Uh, yes, yes—"

Ricia and Kendrick have made love whenever they can. The accounts were never explicit, but the words were often passionate.

"We'll keep you tuned in when we need you, like for an alarm clock," Broberg clipped. "Otherwise we'll cut the circuit."

"But—Look, I never meant to—"

"I know," Scobie sighed. "You're a nice guy and I daresay we're overreacting. Still, that's the way it's got to be. Call us when I told you."

Deep within the grotto, the Pythoness sways on her throne, in the ebb and flow of her orac-

ular dream. As nearly as Ricia and Kendrick can understand what she chants, she tells them to fare westward on the Stag Path until they meet a one-eyed graybeard who will give them further guidance; but they must be wary in his presence, for he is easily angered. They make obeisance and depart. On their way out, they pass the offering they brought. Since they have little with them other than garments and his weapons, the Princess gave the shrine her golden hair. The knight insists that, close-cropped, she remains beautiful.

"Hey, whoops, we've cleared us an easy twenty meters," Scobie said, albeit in a voice which weariness had hammered flat. *At first the journey, through the land of Narce, is a delight.*

His oath afterward had no more life in it. "Another blind alley, seems like." *The old man in the blue cloak and wide-brimmed hat was indeed wrathful when Ricia refused him her favors and Kendrick's spear struck his own aside. Cunningly, he has pretended to make peace and told them what road they should take next. But at the end of it are trolls. The wayfarers elude them and double back.*

"My brain's stumbling around in a swamp, a fog," Scobie groaned. "My busted rib isn't exactly helping, either. If I don't get another nap I'll keep on making misjudgments till we run out of time."

"By all means, Colin," Broberg said. "I'll stand watch and rouse you in an hour."

"What?" he asked in dim surprise. "Why not

join me and have Mark call us as he did before?"—

She grimaced. "No need to bother him. I'm tired, yes, but not sleepy."

He lacked wit or strength to argue. "Okay," he said, stretched his insulating pad on the ice, and toppled out of awareness.

Broberg settled herself next to him. They were halfway to the heights, but they had been struggling, with occasional breaks, for worse than twenty hours, and progress grew more hard and tricky even as they themselves grew more weak and stupefied. If ever they reached the top and spied Danzig's signal, they would have something like a couple of hours' stiff travel to shelter.

Saturn, sun, stars shone through vitryl. Broberg smiled down at Scobie's face. He was no Greek god, and sweat, grime, unshavenness, the manifold marks of exhaustion were upon him, but— For that matter, she was scarcely an image of glamour herself.

Princess Ricia sits by her knight, where he slumbers in the dwarf's cottage, and strums a harp the dwarf lent her before he went off to his mine, and sings a lullaby to sweeten the dreams of Kendrick. When it is done, she passes her lips lightly across his, and drifts into the same gentle sleep.

Scobie woke a piece at a time. "Ricia, beloved," *Kendrick whispers, and feels after her. He will summon her up with kisses—*

He scrambled to his feet, "Judas priest!" She lay unmoving. He heard her breath in his earplugs, before the roaring of his pulse drowned it. The sun glared farther aloft, he could see it had moved, and Saturn's crescent had thinned more, forming sharp thorns at its ends. He forced his eyes toward the watch on his left wrist.

"Ten hours," he choked.

He knelt and shook his companion. "Come, for Christ's sake!" Her lashes fluttered. When she saw the horror on his visage, drowsiness fled from her.

"Oh, no," she said. "Please, no."

Scobie climbed stiffly erect and flicked his main radio switch. "Mark, do you receive?"

"Colin!" Danzig chattered. "Thank God! I was going out of my head from worry."

"You're not off that hook, my friend. We just finished a ten hour snooze."

"What? How far did you get first?"

"To about forty meters' elevation. The going looks tougher ahead than in back. I'm afraid we won't make it."

"Don't *say* that, Colin," Danzig begged.

"My fault," Broberg declared. She stood rigid, fists doubled, features a mask. Her tone was steady. "He was worn out, had to have a nap. I offered to wake him, but fell asleep myself."

"Not your fault, Jean," Scobie began.

She interrupted: "Yes. Mine. Perhaps I can make it good. Take my fuel cell. I'll still have deprived you of my help, of course, but you might survive and reach the boat anyway."

He seized her hands. They did not unclench. "If you imagine I, I could do that—"

"If you don't, we're both finished," she said unbendingly. "I'd rather go out with a clear conscience."

"And what about my conscience?" he shouted. Checking himself, he wet his lips and said fast: "Besides, you're not to blame. Sleep slugged you. If I'd been thinking, I'd have realized it was bound to do so, and contacted Mark. The fact that you didn't either shows how far gone you were yourself. And . . . you've got Tom and the kids waiting for you. Take my cell." He paused. "And my blessing."

"Shall Ricia forsake her true knight?"

"Wait, hold on, listen," Danzig called. "Look, this is terrible, but—oh, hell, excuse me, but I've got to remind you that dramatics only clutter the action. From what descriptions you've sent, I don't see how either of you can possibly proceed solo. Together, you might yet. At least you're rested—sore in the muscles, no doubt, but clearer in the head. The climb before you may prove easier than you think. Try!"

Scobie and Broberg regarded each other for a whole minute. A thawing went through her, and warmed him. Finally they smiled and embraced. "Yeah, right," he growled. "We're off. But first a bite to eat. I'm plain, old-fashioned hungry. Aren't you?" she nodded.

"That's the spirit," Danzig encouraged them. "Uh, may I make another suggestion? I am just a spectator, which is pretty hellish but does give me an overall view. Drop that game of yours."

Scobie and Broberg tautened.

"It's the real culprit," Danzig pleaded.

"Weariness alone wouldn't have clouded your judgment. You'd never have cut me off, and—But weariness and shock and grief did lower your defenses to the point where the damned game took you over. You weren't yourselves when you feel asleep. You were those dream-world characters. They had no reason not to cork off!"

Broberg shook her head violently. "Mark," said Scobie, "you are correct about being a spectator. That means there are some things you don't understand. Why subject you to the torture of listening in, hour after hour? We'll call you back from time to time, naturally. Take care." He broke the circuit.

"He's wrong," Broberg insisted.

Scobie shrugged. "Right or wrong, what difference? We won't pass out again in the time we have left. The game didn't handicap us as we traveled. In fact, it helped, by making the situation feel less gruesome."

"Aye. Let us break our fast and set forth anew on our pilgrimage."

The struggle grew stiffer. "Belike the White Witch has cast a spell on this road," *says Ricia.*

"She shall not daunt us," *vows Kendrick.*

"No, never while we fare side by side, you and I, noblest of men."

A slide overcame them and swept them back a dozen meters. They lodged against a crag. After the flow had passed by, they lifted their bruised bodies and limped in search of a different approach. The place where the geologists's hammer remained was no longer accessible.

"What shattered the bridge?" *asks Ricia.*

"A giant," *answers Kendrick.* "I saw him as I fell into the river. He lunged at me, and we fought in the shallows until he fled. He bore away my sword in his thigh."

"You have your spear that Wayland forged," *Ricia says,* "and always you have my heart."

They stopped on the last small outcrop they uncovered. It proved to be not a shelf but a pinnacle of water ice. Around it glittered sand-ice, again quiescent. Ahead was a slope thirty meters in length, and then the rim, and stars. The distance might as well have been thirty light-years. Whoever tried to cross would immediately sink to an unknown depth.

There was no point in crawling back down the bared side of the pinnacle. Broberg had clung to it for an hour while she chipped niches to climb by with her knife. Scobie's condition had not allowed him to help. If they sought to return, they could easily slip, fall, and be engulfed. If they avoided that, they would never find a new path. Less than two hours' worth of energy abode in their fuel cells. Attempting to push onward while swapping Garcilaso's back and forth could be an exercise in futility.

They settled themselves, legs dangling over the abyss, and held hands and looked at Saturn and at one another.

"I do not think the orcs can burst the iron door of this tower," *Kendrick says,* "but they will besiege us until we starve to death."

"You never yielded up your hope erenow, my knight," *replies Ricia, and kisses his temple.* "Shall we search about? These walls are unutterably ancient. Who knows what relics of wizardry lie forgotten within? A pair of phoenix-feather cloaks, that will bear us laughing through the sky to our home—?"

"I fear not, my darling. Our weird is upon us." *Kendrick touches the spear that leans agleam against the battlement.* "Sad and gray will the world be without you. We can but meet our doom bravely."

"Happily, since we are together." *Ricia's gamin smile breaks forth.* "I did notice that a certain room holds a bed. Shall we try it?"

Kendrick frowns. "Rather should we seek to set our minds and souls in order."

She tugs his elbow. "Later, yes. Besides—who knows?—when we dust off the blanket, we may find it is a Tarnkappe that will take us invisible through the enemy."

"You dream."

Fear stirs behind her eyes. "What if I do?" *Her words tremble.* "I can dream us free if you will help."

Scobie's fist smote the ice. "No!" he croaked. "I'll die in the world that is."

Ricia shrinks from him. He sees terror invade her. "You, you rave, beloved," *she stammers.*

He twisted about and caught her by the arms. "Don't you want to remember Tom and your boys?"

"Who—?"

Kendrick slumps. "I don't know. I have forgotten too."

She leans against him, there on the windy height. A hawk circles above. "The residuum of an evil enchantment, surely. Oh, my heart, my life, cast it from you! Help me find the means to save us." *Yet her entreaty is uneven, and through it speaks dread.*

Kendrick straightens. He lays hand on Wayland's spear, and it is as though strength flows thence, into him. "A spell in truth," *he says. His tone gathers force.* "I will not abide in its darkness, nor suffer it to blind and deafen you, my lady in domnei." *His gaze takes hold of hers, which cannot break away.* "There is but a single road to our freedom. It goes through the gates of death."

She waits, mute and shuddering.

"Whatever we do, we must die, Ricia. Let us fare hence as our own folk."

"I—no—I won't—I will—"

"You see before you the means of your deliverance. It is sharp, I am strong, you will feel no pain."

She bares her bosom. "Then quickly, Kendrick, before I am lost!"

He drives the weapon home. "I love you," he says. *She sinks at his feet.* "I follow you, my darling," *he says, withdraws the steel, braces shaft against stone, lunges forward, falls beside her.* "Now we are free."

"That was . . . a nightmare." Broberg sounded barely awake.

Scobie's voice shook. "Necessary, I think, for both of us." He gazed straight before him, letting Saturn fill his eyes with dazzle. "Else we'd have stayed . . . insane? Maybe not, by definition. But we'd not have been in reality either."

"It would have been easier," she mumbled. "We'd never have known we were dying."

"Would you have preferred that?"

Broberg shivered. The slackness in her countenance gave place to the same tension that was in his. "Oh, no," she said, quite softly but in the manner of full consciousness. "No, you were right, of course. Thank you for your courage."

"You've always had as much guts as anybody, Jean. You just have more imagination than me." Scobie's hand chopped empty space, a gesture of dismissal. "Okay, we should call poor Mark and let him know. But first—" His words lost the cadence he had laid on them. "First—"

Her glove clasped his. "What, Colin?"

"Let's decide about that third unit, Luis'," he said with difficulty, still confronting the great ringed planet. "Your decision, actually, though we can discuss the matter if you want. I will not hog it for the sake of a few more hours. Nor will I share it; that would be a nasty way for us both to go out. However, I suggest you use it."

"To sit beside your frozen corpse?" she replied. "No. I wouldn't even feel the warmth, not in my bones—"

She turned toward him so fast that she nearly fell off the pinnacle. He caught her. "*Warmth!*" she screamed, shrill as the cry of a hawk on the wing. "Colin, we'll take our bones home!"

* * *

"In point of fact," said Danzig, "I've climbed onto the hull. That's high enough for me to see over those ridges and needles. I've got a view of the entire horizon."

"Good," grunted Scobie. "Be prepared to survey a complete circle quick. This depends on a lot of factors we can't predict. The beacon will certainly not be anything like as big as what you had arranged. It may be thin and short-lived. And, of course, it may rise too low for sighting at your distance." He cleared his throat. "In that case, we two have bought the farm. But we'll have made a hell of a try, which feels great by itself."

He hefted the fuel cell, Garcilaso's gift. A piece of heavy wire, insulation stripped off, joined the prongs. Without a regulator, the unit poured its maximum power through the short circuit. Already the strand glowed.

"Are you sure you don't want me to do it, Colin?" Broberg asked. "Your rib—"

He made a lopsided grin. "I'm nonetheless better designed by nature for throwing things," he said. "Allow me that much male arrogance. The bright idea was yours."

"It should have been obvious from the first," she said. "I think it would have been, if we weren't bewildered in our dream."

"M-m, often the simple answers are the hardest to find. Besides, we had to get this far or it wouldn't have worked, and the game helped mightily. . . . Are you set, Mark? Heave ho!"

Scobie cast the cell as if it were a baseball, hard and far through the Iapetan gravity field.

Spinning, its incandescent wire wove a sorcerous web across vision. It landed somewhere beyond the rim, on the glacier's back.

Frozen gases vaporized, whirled aloft, briefly recondensed before they were lost. A geyser stood white against the stars.

"I see you! Danzig yelped. "I see your beacon, I've got my bearing, I'll be on my way! With rope and extra energy units and everything!"

Scobie sagged to the ground and clutched at his left side. Broberg knelt and held him, as if either of them could lay hand on his pain. No large matter. He would not hurt much longer.

"How high would you guess the plume goes?" Danzig inquired, calmer.

"About a hundred meters," Broberg replied after study.

"Uh, damn, these gloves do make it awkward punching the calculator. . . . Well, to judge by what I observe of it, I'm between ten and fifteen klicks off. Give me an hour or a tadge more to get there and find your exact location. Okay?"

Broberg checked gauges. "Yes, by a hair. We'll turn our thermostats down and sit very quiet to reduce oxygen demand. We'll get cold, but we'll survive."

"I may be quicker," Danzig said. "That was a worst case estimate. All right, I'm off. No more conversation till we meet. I won't take any foolish chances, but I will need my wind for making speed."

Faintly, those who waited heard him breathe, heard his hastening footfalls. The geyser died.

They sat, arms around waists, and regarded the glory which encompassed them. After a silence, the man said: "Well, I suppose this means the end of the game. For everybody."

"It must certainly be brought under strict control," the woman answered. "I wonder, though, if they will abandon it altogether—out here."

"If they must, they can."

"Yes. We did, you and I, didn't we?"

They turned face to face, beneath that star-beswarmed, Saturn-ruled sky. Nothing tempered the sunlight that revealed them to each other, she a middle-aged wife, he a man ordinary except for his aloneness. They would never play again. They could not.

A puzzled compassion was in her smile. "Dear Friend—" she began.

His uplifted palm warded her from further speech. "Best we don't talk unless it's essential," he said. "That'll save a little oxygen, and we can stay a little warmer. Shall we try if we can sleep?"

Her eyes widened and darkened. "I dare not," she confessed. "Not till enough time has gone past. Now, I might dream."

GREG BEAR

☐	53172-8	BEYOND HEAVEN'S RIVER	$2.95
☐	53173-6		Canada $3.95
☐	53174-4	EON	$3.95
☐	53175-2		Canada $4.95
☐	53167-1	THE FORGE OF GOD	$4.50
☐	53168-X		Canada $5.50
☐	55971-1	HARDFOUGHT (Tor Double with *Cascade Point* by Timothy Zahn	$2.95
☐	55951-7		Canada $3.95
☐	53163-9	HEGIRA	$3.95
☐	53164-7		Canada $4.95
☐	53165-5	PSYCHLONE	$3.95
☐	53166-3		Canada $4.95

Buy them at your local bookstore or use this handy coupon:
Clip and mail this page with your order.

Publishers Book and Audio Mailing Service
P.O. Box 120159, Staten Island, NY 10312-0004

Please send me the book(s) I have checked above. I am enclosing $______
(please add $1.25 for the first book, and $.25 for each additional book to cover postage and handling. Send check or money order only — no CODs.)

Name ____________________

Address ____________________

City __________ State/Zip __________

Please allow six weeks for delivery. Prices subject to change without notice.

PROSERPINA SPEAKING, PLUTO ORBIT TO MOONBASE ONE

She took a deep breath. "Anyhow, since my last report to you I have sent down one of the smaller probes. It landed on a little hill, one about to be submerged by the just-forming sea. Smacked down next to an ice crag which I'm pretty sure is ammonia and carbon dioxide. Telemetry will tell all. The probe reported to me faithfully until an hour and a half ago, and then . . ." She paused to gather up her courage, imaging old Ben's laugh and Dr. Jensen's frown, even though both her mentors were more than six billion kilometers away, ". . . then, I believe something ate it."

The Tor SF Doubles

A Meeting with Medusa/Green Mars, Arthur C. Clarke/Kim Stanley Robinson • **Hardfought/Cascade Point,** Greg Bear/Timothy Zahn • **Born with the Dead/The Saliva Tree,** Robert Silverberg/Brian W. Aldiss • **No Truce with Kings/Ship of Shadows,** Poul Anderson/Fritz Leiber • **Enemy Mine/Another Orphan,** Barry B. Longyear/John Kessel • **Screwtop/The Girl Who Was Plugged In,** Vonda N. McIntyre/James Tiptree, Jr. • **The Nemesis from Terra/Battle for the Stars,** Leigh Brackett/Edmond Hamilton • **The Ugly Little Boy/The [Widget], the [Wadget], and Boff,** Isaac Asimov/Theodore Sturgeon • **Sailing to Byzantium/Seven American Nights,** Robert Silverberg/Gene Wolfe • **Houston, Houston, Do You Read?/Souls,** James Tiptree, Jr./Joanna Russ • **He Who Shapes/The Infinity Box,** Roger Zelazny/Kate Wilhelm • **The Blind Geometer/The New Atlantis,** Kim Stanley Robinson/Ursula K. Le Guin • **The Saturn Game/Iceborn,** Poul Anderson/Gregory Benford and Paul A. Carter • **The Last Castle/Nightwings,*** Jack Vance/Robert Silverberg • **The Color of Neanderthal Eyes/And Strange at Ecbatan the Trees,*** James Tiptree, Jr./Michael Bishop • **Divide and Rule/The Sword of Rhiannon,*** L. Sprague de Camp/Leigh Brackett

**forthcoming*

GREGORY BENFORD

AND PAUL A. CARTER

ICEBORN

A TOM DOHERTY ASSOCIATES BOOK
NEW YORK

This is a work of fiction. All the characters and events portrayed in this book are fictitious, and any resemblance to real people or events is purely coincidental.

ICEBORN

An earlier version of this novella was published in *Synergy* 3, 1989, under the title "Proserpina's Daughter."

Copyright © 1989 by Abbenford Associates and Paul A. Carter

All rights reserved, including the right to reproduce this book or portions thereof in any form.

A TOR Book
Published by Tom Doherty Associates, Inc.
49 West 24 Street
New York, NY 10010

Cover art by Mark Maxwell

ISBN: 0-812-50277-9 Can. ISBN: 0-812-50269-8

First edition: November 1989

Printed in the United States of America

0 9 8 7 6 5 4 3 2 1

I

Light—pale, blue-cold, little more than starshine—crept over the frozen plains. Dancing blue and green auroral sheets dimmed above. On the Dayside skyline, a turbid yellow stain swelled at the hard brim of the world. Then a sudden, blinding-bright point threw stretched shadows across the hummocked land. The seventy-seven hours' night was over.

Sunlight, waxing yet still wan, laid siege to a rampart of spiky white needles. Temperatures edged imperceptibly further away from absolute zero. This minute change sufficed; the sharp crystalline spearpoints curled, sagged, slumped. Gray vapor rose to meet the tepid dawn. It met even colder, drier air from Darkside that came sliding in on a rushing wind. Rain fell in wobbly dollops.

The Zand woke.

Surface relays activated by the sun sent crisp neural discharges coursing through the coils within its body. The spherical shell which had sealed it from the long night split and retracted. Brittle rods clacked, withdrawing inside, finding fresh socketings in an internal skeleton. Pulpy organs sluggishly made room for the new, active physiology. The Zand turned its still-glazed lenses directly toward the distant hard point of radiance. This prickly stimulus was just enough. Aided by energy hoarded through the bitter night, thick locomotor rings along the Zand's daytime body began to pulse. The great beast moved.

Just before it had gone to sleep the night before, the Zand had marked an outcrop of food-rock and carefully covered it with snow. Now the ever-thickening rain beat upon the cache. The Zand splashed through rivulets to the top of the low knoll, fighting the humming wind that blew toward the dawn. Stiffly the Zand extruded its blower and drove the rest of the damp, melting snow off the outcrop. Then it rested.

Dizziness swept through the long body. The Zand had used too much from its small stock of night-husbanded energy; this was going to be a very near thing. Desperately it scanned the area for the blind life-stirrings that, if present, meant it would live out another day.

There! Black spore cases as hard as the Zand's own night-armor popped open. Atmospheric gas, compressed and pent up all night, blew out the tiny cells that had been locked inside.

Most of them fell on barren ground and died. A few spun in long arcs that landed them on the outcrop where they instantly burrowed in. Mindlessly, ravenously, ecstatically, they ate. From their positive poles hissed the buoyant lifegas the Zand so badly needed. Within their bodies the powerful solvent released by their banqueting reacted with their cell-stuff, yielding other, heavier, gases. They split, dividing to multiply. Wriggling, they squirmed deep into the porous foodrock they fed upon, their growing mass smothering it like a brown carpet.

The Zand edged closer, waited for the right moment—and sucked in deep savory drafts of the zesty life-giving element they gave forth.

The sick, all-but-gone feeling vanished. The furnace of the Zand's own metabolism now fully ignited, and the highly reactive processes that stoked its fires sent waves of health and strength surging along its entire daybody.

For the first time since waking, the Zand reared fully upright. Its chilled mind now fully unlocked and aware, it trumpeted a hymn of praise to Lightgiver. That majestic Source of all life now floated entirely clear of the horizon, still shrouded in rising, swirling blue-white vapors and the driving early-morning rain.

Something solid swept out of the cloaking pearly mists into the Zand's field of perception. The Zand tensed to fight. This must be a Flapper riding the turbulent air currents toward the outcrop in order to steal from the foodfarm.

But the object that came thumping and tumbling to rest at the edge of the foodrock, sending cold steam puffing up from where it lay, was—*new*. Alien. Round like Lightgiver, or like the Zand itself at night, but small, smooth, hot. In its polished surface the Zand saw itself, grotesquely distorted.

The Zand hungrily reversed its blower-organ and vacuumed the thing into its forward orifice. Then came the first shock.

The object was a tough, heavy lump, far worse than a large Flapper. Dull pain throbbed through the alimentary tract.

The Zand's first impulse was to spew the offensive object forth. But the Zand had not survived night after night to greet Lightgiver by merely obeying its impulses. Therefore, it hunched closer to the outcrop and scooped up a generous helping of spicy Eaters. At once their furious body chemistry gave aid to its own. The fuming corrosive that was kindled in their first digestive stage bit into the strange sphere.

The Zand's inward discomfort transmuted into a heady glow of well-being. Strange, vibrant tastes rippled through its body. Nothing except Self-merge had ever given it such joy.

The rain curtain of wobbly drops lifted, unveiling the hot glory of Lightgiver's face. Ruby meltfluid rose high enough to slap at the crusty outcrop. The Zand, its digestion complete, felt flooded as never before with power and hope. Turning its back to the wind, it pushed away from the colony of Eaters into the new-formed sea. It stopped breathing, to store its surplus of lifegas and burngas against a time of greater need. For now the alternating cycles of energy in its coils would suffice. Broadcasting a joyous morning psalm, the Zand swam with great ring-surge strokes toward the brightening day.

II

Shanna West put on the last movement of Beethoven's Fifth and turned up the gain.

Ludwig von Cornball, they called him back at Moonbase One. And she could well visualize Dr. Jensen tut-tutting at this latest display of childish dramatization. But Moonbase and Jensen were electromagnetically five hours and twenty minutes away; physically they were more than a *year* away.

For the time being, within the survival limits set by the spacecraft, she could do what she damned well pleased. With a happy sigh, Shanna relaxed into her hammock and gave herself up to the symphony's triumphant chords of victory.

Pluto was lightly banded in pale gray and salmon red save where Charon cast its huge gloomy shadow. Massive ice sheets spread like pearly blankets from both poles. Ridges ribbed the frozen methane ranges. The equatorial land was a flinty, scarred band, hemmed in by the oppressive ice. The planet turned almost imperceptibly in its diurnal cycle at the solar system's edge.

Observers on Earth had thought Pluto, Charon, and the sun could only line up for an eclipse every 124 years—but in 2029, to the utter surprise of Earthside astronomers, both the satellite's orbit and the planet's axis had begun to drift. By the time the Pluto mission was launched in 2044 Charon was eclipsing the sun regularly each Plutonian day.

Strange, thought Shanna. And typical of Pluto and its moon that they should thus confound Earth's experts—who had warned her that this remote, small, cold world would be dull.

But those glorious filmy auroras! They alone were worth the trip, even though a beetle-browed Congressperson would hardly have agreed.

She let the view absorb her for a last few moments. Her fellow crew, Albers and Parsons and Ukizi, would have each had a specialist's fascination in the frigid vistas. But they had all died in the hibernation tanks, a dumb technical malfunction she could not have caught; victims of last-minute idiotic cost-cutting in the tanks' design—the old, life-hazarding penny-pinching that had disgraced space exploration since the legendary *Challenger* botch. Bitterness flooded her, together with an irrational but real spasm of personal guilt. What a scientific feast those three would have made of this bleakly beautiful place!

Now she, not the theoretician of the crew but the tech type who could repair anything, had to cobble together a scientific analysis. The three frozen corpses she carried in storage demanded her best effort; that had been why she refused to abort the mission and return quickly to Earthside after she broke the news. She had a debt to pay to her older—and, she thought, *better*—comrades.

And now she had to confess that the original goal that had brought the four of them out to Pluto was lost. She resolved to be relentlessly cheerful; that would be the only way to get through the broadcast. It was going to be tough, breaking the bad-news Earthside on top of the previous news of the deaths.

Better to give them some solid hard science stuff first, then. Soften up the tech types for the disappointment. Sweeten the pill.

The symphony ended. A heartbeat later a musical chime—rigged by Shanna in protest against the usual peremptory beeping alarms—told her that the data gathered since *Proserpina*'s last radio contract had now been encoded and kicked back toward Moonbase One. She tapped a key, giving herself a voice channel.

"As we agreed, I am adding my own verbal comments to the data I have just sent you." (The had *not* agreed; many of the Pluto Mission Control engineers, wedded to the mathematical slang and NASA's jawbone acronyms, felt commentary was subjective and useless . . . let the lab teams back home interpret the data.)

"Pluto is a much livelier place than we ever imagined. There's weather, for one thing. Looks like it's a product of the planet's six-day rotation. Turns out the melting/freezing point of methane is crucial. The mean temperature is just high enough that nitrogen and argon stay gaseous, giving Pluto a thin atmosphere. Of course, the ammonia and CO_2 are solid as rock. Methane, though, can go either way. Earthside observers found methane frost on the surface as long ago as 1976—remember?—and methane icecaps in 1987. They speculated even then that some of it might start to thaw as the planet approached perihelion. Well, it did—and still does, every Plutonian morning. Even better, the CH_4 doesn't just sublime, as it was supposed to because of the low atmospheric pressure—it *melts*. Then it freezes at night.

"Meanwhile on the dark side a great 'heat sink,' like the one over Antarctica on Earth, moves slowly across the planet as it turns, radiating heat into space and pressing down a column of cold air—I mean, of even *colder* air. From its lowest, coldest point, adiabatic winds flow out toward the day side. At the sunset line they meet sun-warmed air, and it snows. On the sunrise side they meet sunlight and melting methane ice, and it rains. So we've got a perpetual storm front moving at the edge of the night side, and another that travels with the sunrise."

As she warmed to her subject, all pretense at impersonal scientific discourse faded from Shanna's voice; she could not filter out her excitement that verged on a kind of love. She paused, watching the swirling blizzards at twilight's edge and, on the dawn side, the great racks of cloud. Although admittedly no Jupiter, this planet—*her* planet—could put on quite a show. Then she remembered her lost crewmen and continued:

"The result is a shallow sea of methane that moves slowly around the world, following the sun. Since methane doesn't expand as it freezes, like water"—*they* know that, she thought bitterly, but for the skeptics back home who still wonder whether a kid could carry on the mission I'd better show that *I* know it—"I'm sure it's all slush a short way below the surface, and solid ice from there down. But the sea isn't stagnant, because of what the satellite in its synchronous orbit is doing. As big as Charon is, and as close to the planet as it's gotten since its orbit shifted, it makes a permanent tidal bulge directly underneath it. And *that* travels around from daylight to darkness also. So sea currents form, and flow, and freeze. On the night side, the tidal pull puts stress on the various ices, and they hump up and buckle into pressure ridges. Like the ones in Antarctica, but *much* bigger."

She bit her lip. Now for the hard part.

She'd rehearsed this a dozen times, but still the words stuck in her throat. After all, she hadn't come here to do close-up planetology. An unmanned orbital mission could have done that nicely. Shanna had come in search of life.

Twenty-two years before, the life-is-everywhere advocates had suffered a rough rollback at the hands of nature. The first roboprobe which landed on Saturn's moon, Titan, had found strings of crystal that emitted tantalizing, ordered, low-frequency electromagnetic waves. Attempts to decipher them seemed to yield a complex array of possible interpretations. The mathematical and linguistic communities invested enormous energy over a full decade to ferret out significance in the blizzard of incoming data from the strange, multicolored crystals. A second and third probe contributed to this flood, and it all came to a bitter end.

The third probe sank deep sensors. Spectral analysis showed that rather than elegant crystal poetry or alien communal song, the Titan emissions were refracted seismic tremors from deep inside the icy moon. The apparent order of them came from an interweave of tidal forces and crustal oscillations, teamed with a cyclic weather pattern in the thick Titan air of torpid methane huricanes.

The fortunes and careers consumed in proving that the glossy crystals were *not* alive then made further pursuit of life in the Solar System a dead, discredited issue. High-minded but exaggerated claims now came back to haunt the present generation of planetary astronomers. The space industrialists were quite eager to help this along, pointing out that the same amount invested in an economical, steady ion drive would have helped open the asteroids to extensive mining and colonization.

True enough, but like most workhorses, the ion pusher could serve many masters. Once built, its high efficiency made possible missions to the far rim of Sol's domain.

Even so, the planetary science community would not have been able to extract the money for the outer-system study. But then nature—having suckered them on their last bet—showed an enticing new gamble.

The new generation radio telescopes, the Space Array, had just completed its thousand-kilometer span. It detected very low frequency radio waves from Pluto. This time, the code developed to wrestle with Titan's elegant mumbo jumbo, Wiseguy, suggested true intelligent origin. But the signals were refracted and damped by the plasma streams billowing forth from the sun, so the Space Array near Earth got only glimmerings of the Plutonian emission. It was enticing—even convincing—to the converted. That had led Shanna to this crucial moment. She made herself say,

"The . . . the orderly emissions that the Space Array saw, and that I've been monitoring for the past year . . . well . . ." She took a deep breath. "I've proven they're natural. No intelligent signals after all."

She paused, held her breath almost as if she expected a chorus of sighs, groans, shouts. But the community that had hoped she would find a striking refutation to the nay-sayers . . . that band was clustered around a viewscreen an unimaginable distance away.

"I'm sorry, but that's the truth. I ran the Wiseguy program continually, hoping the transmissions were beyond the program's insight. Not so. The entire Plutonian magnetosphere somehow cooperates in sending those devilishly intricate signals. I've been holding off telling you . . . because . . . well, I wish I could say that I was trying to discover the cause. And I *was* . . . but mostly, I just didn't want to give up hope. Now that I'm here, and have all of Pluto to study, I can finally pass the word. No aliens . . . sorry . . ."

She blinked rapidly. This was a torturous confessional, but she had to do it. She coughed, excused herself self-consciously from people who would not hear the cough until five and a half hours hence. Then she made her voice more brisk, scientific.

"Mind you, the emissions *are* interesting. There's some driver in the whole magnetosphere, and I think I've found it. A current is flowing in from farther out, 'way *'way* beyond Pluto's orbit. Maybe from the Oort Cloud of junk left over from the formation of the Solar System, out where the comets come from."

To her ears, this chatty bravado rang false, but maybe it would play better back Earthside . . .

"I've detected signs that plasma winds out here are driven across the solar magnetic fields. That creates an electric field, which pushes some pretty huge currents in toward Pluto. And little old Pluto packs a wallop, too. It's got a large magnetic field of its own, lying nearly perpendicular to its spin axis—I sent you the stats on this already. It's a generator, like Uranus. Weaker than Uranus, sure—but out here in this neck of the woods, any energy source is big news."

She stopped, sensing the skepticism these last sentences would provoke six hours from now. She sighed. This was even harder than she'd feared. Her mind kept lurching off on tangents, spilling out scientific data and ideas, but behind the facade she was a fountain of emotion. Could they tell?

She took a deep breath and changed the subject. "Also, there's a lot more free hydrogen than a planet this little ought to be able to hold. At some spots on the day side I've measured gaseous carbon dioxide, although it all ought to be frozen. There are some strange spectral lines . . ."

Shanna caught herself before saying what those lines seemed to show. She was not ready to make that leap of faith; not yet. "Anyhow, since my last report to you I have sent down one of the smaller probes. It landed on a little hill, one about to be submerged by the just-forming sea. Smacked down next to an ice crag which I'm pretty sure is ammonia and carbon dioxide. Telemetry will tell all. The probe reported to me faithfully until an hour and a half ago, and then . . ." she paused to gather up her courage, imagining old Ben's laugh and Dr. Jensen's frown, even though both her mentors were more than six billion kilometers away, ". . . then, I believe something ate it."

III

Lightgiver's rays broke through thinning clouds as the rains of morning ended. Still the Zand swam tirelessly on toward Rendezvous with the others of its kind. It had not felt this strong for many, many long days. When it found another of the zands and they Self-merged, as usually happened before any day's end, there might even be a Birthing this time . . .

Tearing pain lashed at the Zand's underside. The hooked head of a Borer twisted into the hole it had made; the Borer's tail whipped the sea into foam, powering the parasite's body around and around and *in*, deep and terribly wounding.

As the pain passed the threshold of bearability and faintness began, the Zand's automatic neural defense system took over. Lifegas and burngas, stored in compression chambers along its sides, vented into the central canal. A neural impulse connector parted, creating a spark. Lifegas and burngas ignited in a jet of searing fire. The Zand lifted up and away, out of the sea.

The Borer clung on, its narrow winding body writhing and lashing against the much larger Zand. The living rocket left a trail of ivory as the product of the lifegas-burngas reaction froze. Air pressure dropped, sucking the Borer from its hold. It fell into the sea.

Air rushing past soothed the wound. Lightgiver be thanked for fast reactions, the Zand thought. It trimmed its course to swing back down toward the sea, even though—still charged up with those incredible rejuvenating energies from the strange thing it had eaten earlier that morning—it was tempted to remain airborne. But it would need its lifegas later on, should there be no food at Rendezvous; for by now most of the rockfood on the world's day side was submerged.

Again it sang a canticle to Lightgiver, weaving in with its general praise to the almighty Nourisher of the world its own specific thanks at having been spared for further life. The Zand vowed to the sky that it would teach young zands to revere Lightgiver's holy name, should Lightgiver see fit to grant it a Birthing.

A faint broadcast signal interrupted its meditations. The Zand responded with its own distinctive pulses, and received in return a conversational rush of joy from another zand. Old One had evidently survived the night again.

By mutual agreement both zands sealed themselves and expended enough of their precious lifegas to lift and float them just above the surface of the sea, resting.

"I am glad you have survived another day," the Zand began, as was proper for a younger person to say.

"And I also, that we greet one another. We may not look forward to an indefinite number of such days," Old One replied.

Life on their ever-changing world was precarious, but Old One's tone implied something far more comprehensive and profound. Intellectual curiosity—with an undernote of fear—prevailed over the deference due to age. "Explain," the Zand begged.

"Think back, youngling. Think back to your last Birthing. How did Lightgiver look in the sky?"

The Zand pondered. Self-merge and Birthing were such all-absorbing experiences that one did not, at the time, pay much attention to one's surroundings. Not even to Lightgiver? the Zand's conscience prodded, and a twinge of shame filled it for its evident lack of devotion. And then it remembered. "Lightgiver was brighter—and warmer—and . . . and . . ."

"And *larger*?" Old One prompted.

"And larger, yes."

"Now let me share something with you before I die." Old One brushed aside its companion's polite protests. "No; I cannot go through many more days and nights of gorge and sleep, gorge and sleep. So attend me while you can, and tell this to the other zands. I *am* the Old

One; probably the oldest in the world. And I have watched the skies with care. Beyond the cycle of dark and light which we know every night and day is a far longer cycle. We have no proper way to measure it. But I have thought this out, and I can tell you that Lightgiver moves in and out, from Its greatest width to Its narrowest, in more than fourteen thousand of our short cycles of night and day. I myself have seen two of these greater cycles, and I can tell you that for most of that time, while Lightgiver is at Its farthest and coldest, the ice does not melt, and there is no sea, and even in full day all life sleeps."

This was a dark idea, as dark as the world's somber night side itself.

The Zand sensed a weariness in Old One's soul, so it tried to express cheer: "And then Lightgiver comes back, and is close and warm, and life wakes again?"

"Yes. But in the first of these long cycles through which I have lived we numbered eight thousand zands. We lost some to Borers and Flappers and starvation, and of course each night—then as now—some never made it through to the morning. Once in that cycle came a great raid from Darkside—yes, youngling, the story told in the epic chant is true. Intelligences exist back there, feeding on Lightgiver knows what—and we drove them off in the terrible battle of which that legend tells, with much loss of life."

"But . . . the Birthings?"

"Almost enough to maintain our numbers. But not quite. And so there remained more than seven thousand of us when that long cycle reached the point of daytime freeze."

"You all slept?"

"Yes, and Lightgiver shrank to Its smallest size—I assume, for of course I could not watch during the frozen time. Then Lightgiver began to grow again, to the point at which It could again give us warmth and zest. But as the second cycle began, fewer of us awoke. *How many zands are there today?*"

The daily Rendezvous insured that all of them knew. "Yesterday there were three thousand four hundred and forty-one."

"Half what there were before the last long freeze. And Lightgiver bestows less warmth and light every day. Your personal experience is that of other zands: Self-merge leads to Birthing only when our world is most warm."

"So we do not grow in numbers sufficient to replace ourselves?"

"Yes, and then the long cold time takes a further toll. If three thousand of us live until the next great freeze begins, far fewer than that number will wake for the start of the next warming cycle. Fewer still will see its end. A day will come, therefore, when no zands at all will meet at Rendezvous, ever again."

Terror shook the younger Zand. "And if *none* of us wake and feed, who will be there to sing Lightgiver's praises?"

"The Flappers and the Borers, perhaps," Old One savagely replied. Then, more gently, "Go, youngling; I have told you. Go to Rendezvous!

Tell the others! May you have good Self-merge, with a Birthing and many young."

With a hiss the Zand deflated, dropped into the sea, and began almost desperately to swim. Old One, buoyed by lifegas, floated and pondered.

IV

A red light came on in the middle of the Pluto Project Administrator's desk.

Benjamin Rabi crushed out his cigar stub, hurriedly shoved it and the ashtray into a bottom desk drawer, and turned up the air circulator. In a few moments Dr. Jensen would be walking in, and there was no point in adding to the psychiatrist's expectable irritation. To the traditional medical and moral arguments against smoking, Ben reflected, had lately been added a snob objection as well: tobacco use had come to be associated (by Euro-Americans) with the Third World's urban hells, where people smoked because it was the only pleasure they could afford.

The sealable double door swung open and Hilge Jensen stepped over the threshold. She was in her hospital whites, not her office wear, which was always a sign of trouble. She opened her mouth and the Administrator defused the situation as best he could by chorusing with her the exact words he knew she was going to say: "I'm worried about Shanna."

They had opened countless conversations just that way over the past year. Even Hilge laughed at thus being trapped into a cliché.

Then she frowned. "Shanna's scheduled to contact us again—timed for tonight's press conference, of all things!"

"Look, Hilge—she sent that first message at 0500 our time, and then knocked off for sleep or exercise, I expect. We got it at 1020. I replied to her at noon, and against my better judgment I spoke the lines *you* wrote for me—practically word for word, right? She got my transmission late this afternoon. The mail service between here and there being what it is, that's about the best I can do."

"But God only knows what's coming down the road from Pluto with her next report."

Rabi said flatly, "You really think she's cracking up, don't you?"

"But she thinks there's *life* on Pluto!" Dr. Jensen exploded.

Mildly, the Administrator asked, "And what if there is?"

"Oh, come off it, Ben. Remember Titan, for God's sake!" Jensen paused for breath, but Rabi remained silent, letting her work off steam. "You know what an obsession Pluto has always been for Shanna. She's just indulging in wish-fulfillment fantasy."

"You don't *know* that."

"Look, consider her personality profile. Smart as a whip, and she paid for it in the usual coinage—isolated with the elite in school, socially a bit slow. Raised by a grandmother because neither of her own, self-fulfilling parents could be bothered. So she learned early to live alone and like it. Takes on a late-teenage persona when under pressure because that's the mode she used before she started astronaut training. Solitary tech interests, which she covers in social settings with a jaunty air, exuberance masking anxiety."

"Sure, but we knew she could fit into a two-woman, two-man crew. Her place in the social dynamics was well researched."

"And now she's *alone*. She's reverted back to an old pattern, the bright-eyed kid personality—I mean, listen to that broadcast! It's loaded with false voice signatures! And along with it comes the early idealism. She *wants* there to be life on Pluto. There aren't any green men or red princesses on Mars, but she's bound there'll be something like them on *her* planet. And when people start acting out their fantasies—"

He flared. "So what are we supposed to do? You can't give her word-association tests when it's five hours between the first word and her response, and another five hours before you can throw her the next word!"

Actually, Jensen could, by giving her all the questions at once and getting all the answers back in the same order ten hours later. But Ben knew, and he knew Hilge knew, that would not be clinically the same. Sensing this objection, Dr. Jensen took a different tack:

"Resuscitation from the long cryogenic sleep may have muddled her. Order her to take medication."

Hilge's argument began to fall into a pattern he had heard before, drugs as panacea, and he tuned out. Pluto, he mused. The name conjured up either horror: the stern, just, and unforgiving Roman god of Hell—or low humor: Mickey Mouse's dog.

Yet Shanna had wanted to go there for as long as they had known her. Other little girls' idols had included holomovie hunks and vidsong stars; hers had started and ended with Clyde Tombaugh, the gangly farm kid from Kansas with his homemade telescope who had gone out to the Lowell Observatory early in the previous century and found Pluto in the first place. Dr. Jensen was only the latest in a long line of child specialists, school guidance counselors, and other psychosnoops who had pestered Shanna all her short life with the question "Why?"

The problem for those skeptical therapists and soul-probers had been that Shanna was not, and never had been, unfriendly or antisocial. A quick, lithe athlete, she had played on school teams with all the give-and-take and intuitive awareness of others that such play requires. She had made friends, but on her own terms and not because she couldn't bear to be alone. So the "psychodynamicists" skipped "Why Pluto?" and went directly to "Why do you want to be away for so long?"

Shanna could have reminded her interrogators of Henry Thoreau or of the undeniably great Greta Garbo, but in the twenty-forties that just wouldn't have done. The moral authorities now held that solitude is at best selfish: "If hiking in the woods is so much fun, why not share it?"—and at worst a vice: "Just what are you trying to hide?" Ultimately, Administrator Rabi had overruled the psychiatrist: "Shanna loves it, she wants it, and of all the thousands who applied, she's the best we've got."

The red light came on again, interrupting Rabi's musings and Jensen's monologue. "Hell. That damned new press secretary. He insisted on seeing me before we go on the air."

Jensen shifted gears; her voice became low, slow, and grim. "I know. *I* asked him to be here. Shanna's delusion is also, unfortunately, part of a much larger problem. I'll let him fill you in."

Harvell Swain chose that moment to walk in. Tripping over the threshold on his way through—he was a recent Earthside import, not yet used to lunar doors or the lunar energy-saving walk—he came up to the desk, nodding formally to both Hilge and Ben. "Mr. Administrator; Dr. Jensen. I have come here to tell you that the press conference this evening must be called off."

"Something the matter technically?" Ben countered.

"No. From that standpoint everything is go, as they used to say. But we can't air that report from Astronaut West."

"What do you mean, *we* can't?" the Administrator roared. "Listen—five years we've been sweating out this mission. *Five years!* And after three deaths, people know *Proserpina* got there okay and with only the junior officer piloting her. Some politicians are still calling the whole thing a boondoggle, and using the deaths of Ukizi and Albers and Parsons to say 'told you so.' We've got to have something to show for it, *now*."

"That's exactly the point!" Swain shot back, unexpectedly bold. "Shanna herself said those magnetopheric emissions are natural. So—to have aliens turn up just now? Just when Congress, reacting to those useless and expensive deaths, is about to scuttle the new, faster Orion-drive spacecraft that could get to Pluto in three months? It's too neat, Mr. Administrator. They aren't going to believe her. And if you try to back her up they won't believe you, either."

The press secretary subsided, winded. Then he wound himself up for another try. "Look, Mr. Rabi. I've given this thing all I've got. I laid a lot of groundwork on Earth before coming up here. Human-interest stories about the Project, the works. 'Outer darkness defied for a dream by plucky young girl . . .' "

"Young woman," Hilge automatically corrected.

"No, *girl*, damn it; it makes better PR. Intrepid explorer of our last frontier, only this one's a sexy chick. It made good copy—*good* copy."

And you almost had me until you said that,

Ben mentally replied. Thank the good Lord for big mouths, sometimes. Aloud he observed, with an edge of sarcasm: "You realize, don't you, Mr. Swain, that we have here more than an oral report? Shanna has sent us data, plenty of it—which I have already begun sending down to the *New York Times* database . . . also to the BBC."

Surprisingly, the stereotypically meek and other-directed PR man stood his ground. "And *you* realize, don't you, sir, that data nowadays can very effectively be faked? *That's* what they will think down there."

So much spunk all of a sudden? What, Ben wondered, *does he know politically from Earthside that I don't? What have the superpower governments been up to?*

Time to take the offensive. Benjamin Rabi stood up to his full height, which was considerable; a ploy he rarely had to use. "Look, there's this religion that broke away from my own a couple of thousand years ago, and it and mine haven't always gotten along. But its founder once said, 'You shall know the truth and the truth shall make you free.' Hell, if we can't stick with that, civilization—*scientific* civilization, Dr. Jensen—might as well go out of business. We are going on this evening as scheduled, and take our chances with whatever Shanna has to say."

Appropriately the squawk box on his desk announced: "Ten minutes, Mr. Administrator."

V

The Pluto Mission Control auditorium was jammed. Applause spattered across the tiered seats as Rabi and Jensen came in from the back of the stage, with an apprehensive Swain a few steps to the rear. Behind them an enhanced image of Pluto as *Proserpina* had seen it from a million kilometers out filled the large screen.

The Administrator acknowledged the applause with a short wave of the hand. The cheers were for Shanna, he knew, not for him. He stepped into the chalkmarked area staked out for the holocrameras' focus. Uncomfortably he became aware of the unseen eyes of Earth's billions a light-second and a half away.

"Ladies and gentleman," he began, "we have exciting news from Pluto tonight. At 1030 this morning, GMT, which is also our local time here at Moonbase One"—that it was again called Greenwich Mean Time reflected the UK's surprising political comeback since the turn of the millennium—"we received Astronaut West's first report. Tonight she speaks to us again, and this time you are going to hear her in person. She's over six billion kilometers away from us—that's three point six billion miles for those of you who go in for nostalgia" (the line got a ripple of light laughter in the hall) "and it won't be in supersound. But I think we all want to hear what she has to say." His eye caught the second hand of the big wall clock, closing in on 9—not a digital readout coming up on 2100, another (and expensive) concession to nostalgia—and, timing his last words to end one second before the hour, he said: "All right, Shanna, come in."

The words the young astronaut had spoken from Pluto orbit hours before came booming in, overamplified—and immediately covering them, a dry wash of static. "Damn solar flares," muttered Swain, becoming once again the electronics professional. As the interference continued, people stirred restlessly in their seats. And then the distortion stopped, and the first word from Shanna West that came in loud and clear at Moonbase One and on Earth was ". . . life.

"I'm sure of it!" the woman's fresh, youthful voice exulted. "I matched every molecular combination in the library's memory against it. The *only* compound that even came close was B-chlorophyll. So these are not only plants, they're photosynthetic ones. Back when Pluto was considered more interesting"—she couldn't keep an edge of sarcasm out of her voice—"some hackers at the JPL worked out a series of biochemical reactions that theoretically *could* work here. It turns out they *do*. *But*—they're powered far less by Pluto's distant sun than by electrodynamic coupling with the Oort Cloud's inner ring. The plants combine ammonia ice with carbon dioxide ice and get free hydrogen, carbon, and nitric acid. Then the nitric acid and the carbon recombine, releasing more free hydrogen plus CO_2 and nitrogen—and that's where the animals come in!"

Her voice lilted on "animals" and the word sent a buzz through the crowd.

"They're methanogens. You have a few methanogenic microorganisms on Earth, where—according to some work back in the 1980s, by John Olson and others, on Earth's earliest biosphere—they branched off three and a half billion years ago. Then they got pushed off to the ecological edge of things. Here they're the main show. They recombine the hydrogen and CO_2 released by the plants into free oxygen and methane. They store some of the hydrogen in their bodies, and then they can inflate themselves like hydrogen balloons. I watched two of them floating above the sea that way, apparently just passing the time of day."

Rabi smiled. Nobody, not even that idiot press secretary, could believe she was making *this* up.

"They also store the oxygen, and they can combine it with hydrogen like old-fashioned rocket fuel. I saw one of them escape a predator of some kind by gracefully jetting up through the air, while its exhaust froze behind it and fell into the sea."

"*Really*, now!" Jensen snorted. Ben Rabi hoped that jibe hadn't gone out on the air to Earth. He would have shot her a frown, but he was still on camera.

With uncanny premonition, Shanna's tone turned a shade argumentative: "Yes, a predator. This evidently is a complete, balanced planetary ecology. But I don't think the one that got my first data-gatherer was just a beast. From the readings I was able to get before the hull dissolved, I think the probe was being eaten by nitric acid—which the plants produce but the animals don't. So the creature was employing a plant process, not necessary for its own metabolism, to 'smelt' my probe—and that's awfully close to tool-using. There's not only life on Pluto; there's *intelligent* life!"

The Pluto Project Administrator listened, awed. Then Shanna shocked him. "So much I have been able to learn of this life by remote observation. Now, obviously, I shall have to go down there myself. By the time you hear these words I'm speaking"—Shanna's voice rose in almost childlike delight—"I'll be on my way to Pluto!"

Her voice softened. "I hope the rest of you out there won't mind a personal note. It *is* risky, I guess, and if I don't make it back—good-bye, Dr. Jensen; good-bye, Ben. I really do love you both." And after that, from distant Plutonian space came only a whispering hiss.

As soon as the cameras went off Hilge

growled, "You didn't give her permission to do that!" A growing hubbub filled the hall.

"And I didn't say she couldn't."

Shanna, Shanna, who's like the daughter I never had—take care out there, kid. It's all in your hands now.

VI

The mile-long ice ridge rose out of the sea like a great gray reef. Like its Earthly analogy, it teemed with life. Quilt-patches of vivid blue-green and carrot orange spattered its natural pallor. Out of those patches spindly trunks stretched toward the mid-morning sun; at their tips crackled bright blue St. Elmo's fire. Great violet-hued flying things swooped lazily in and out among them to feed, or alighted at the shoreline and folded themselves, waiting. The sky, even at Pluto's mid-morning, remained a dark backdrop for the gauzy auroral curtains.

Shanna dropped the lander closer. Her legs were cramped from sitting in the small craft's pilot chair, and her bones ached from the unaccustomed surges of chemical propulsion.

She blinked, suddenly alarmed. The drive below her ran red-hot.

Now here was a problem *nobody* on the mission team, for all their contingency planning, had foreseen.

Her rocket-assisted deceleration was bound to incinerate many of the life forms in this fragile ecosystem. Even after she had made planetfall, the vehicle might be too hot for any native animals to approach—not to mention possibly scalding them when the ices near them suddenly boiled away.

Damn it all! In so skimpy an energy environment, how could there be so *many* of them?

Should she go out in her personal armor? The briefers had warned her never, never to use it on the planetary surface. In vacuum it radiated slowly enough that its heater could cope, but if its underside actually touched the frigid ground the heat transfer would be too fast even for its sophisticated insulation.

Her feet would freeze in her boots, then the rest of her. Even for the lander's heavily insulated shock-absorber legs, they had told her, it would be touch-and-go. And the armor also, from the viewpoint of a native Plutonian, must seem a hot, untouchable furnace. "Taking me to your leader is not going to be easy," Shanna said aloud.

Her keen eyes picked out a patch of dark blue-gray down by the shore of the methane sea. Delicately she worked the attitude jets to swing over and take a closer look. She brought up the visual magnification. In detail it looked like rough beach shingle; tidal currents during the twenty-two hours since dawn had dropped some kind of gritty detritus—not one of the ices, apparently—at sea's edge. Nothing would grow there. It was flatter at that place than up on the ridge's knife-edge, which also seemed relatively free of life. This, she decided, would do.

Skillfully, gingerly, Shanna maneuvered down. She almost envied those pioneer astronauts who had first touched the ground on Luna three-quarters of a century ago, backed up by a constant stream of advice, or at least comment, from Houston. On second thought, no, damn it . . . she could do without all that back-seat driving.

With a jar, the lander thumped down on Pluto. Startlingly, sparks spat between its feet and the ground just before touchdown. There must be a *lot* of electricity running around out there, she thought, fervently thanking the designers for all that redundant insulation.

The legs creaked as they took up the shock. The little spacecraft bounced back and down again. The lander stood like one of H. G. Wells's Martian walking-machines, splay-footed and swaying.

One of the movable videolenses was supposed to turn and look directly down—there, that one. The viewframe picked out sharp, angular pebbles and sparkling dust. Rocks? Neil Armstrong and the classic first off-Earth mission came to mind; she had better gather some. She activated the scoop, and the first sample of the ninth planet's soil rattled into the storage bin.

Then Shanna sat there, frustrated. Just what was she going to do?

She tried the wide-band receiver. Happily, she found that the frequencies first logged by her lost, devoured probe were full of traffic. Confusing; each of the beasts—for she was sure it was they—seemed to be broadcasting on all waves at once. Most of the signals were weak, swamped in background noise that sounded like an old AM radio picking up a nearby high-tension line. One, however, came roaring in like a pop music station. Shanna adjusted the inductance tuner, a simple rig not unlike the station selectors the better class of radios had boasted during, say, World War Two.

That pattern—yes! It had to be. Quickly she compared it with the probe-log she'd had the wit to bring down with her. These were the "call letters" of the very beast whose breakfast snack had been her first evidence that the planet held life.

The signal boomed louder, and she turned back the gain. She decided to try the radio direction-finder.

Why, the thing was practically on top of her! If Pluto's lords of creation were all swimming in toward this island ridge for lunch, obviously this one was going to get here first. Fired up by all those vitamins from the lost probe? she wondered.

Suddenly excited, Shanna peered out to sea—and there it was. Only a roiling, frothing wave at first, like a ship's bow wave or a cut-off snippet of surf. Then she saw its great, segmented, open-ended hollow tube of a body, with a sheen somewhere between mother-of-pearl and burnished brass. Why, it was *huge*. For the first time it hit her that when this creature's peers all converged on this spot, it was going to be like sitting smack in the middle of a dinosaur convention.

Too late to back out now. What would her three dead crewmates have done? She powered up the small lifeboat transmitter and tuned it to the signal she was receiving from seaward, though with her equipment she could not duplicate its creative chaos of wavelengths.

For its personal identification sign the beast seemed to use a simple CW pulse, like Morse code. Easy enough to simulate. After a couple of dry-run hand exercises to get with the rhythm of it, Shanna sent the creature a duplicate of its own ID.

The result was astonishing. The Plutonian's internal rocket engine fired a bright orange plume against the sky's black. It shot straight up in the air, paused, and plunged back. Its splash sent waves rolling up the beach; the farthest tongue of fluid broke against the lander's most seaward leg. The living cylinder lay there, half in, half out, as if paralyzed.

Had she terrified it? Made it panic?

Cautiously, Shanna tried the signal again. It *would* give you quite a turn, she realized, if you'd just gotten as far in your philosophizing as "I think, therefore I am," and then heard a thin, toneless duplicate of your own voice give back an exact echo.

Her second signal prompted a long, suspenseful silence. Then, hesitantly—shyly?—the being repeated the call after her.

Shanna let out her breath in a long, shuddering sigh. She hadn't realized she was holding it. *The Eagle has landed,* she told her long-gone grandmother. Then she instructed DIS, the primary computer orbiting Pluto aboard *Proserpina,* to run the one powerful program Pluto Mission Control had never expected her to have to use: the translator, Wiseguy.

The creation of that program climaxed an argument that had raged for a century, ever since Whitehead and Russell had scrapped the old syllogistic logic of Aristotle in favor of a far more powerful method—sufficient, they believed, to subsume the whole of science, perhaps the whole of human cognition.

Can all language be translated into logically rigorous sentences, relating to one another in a configuration of structures one may call a system? If so, one could easily program a computer loaded with one language to search for another language's equivalent of those structures. Or, as many linguists and anthropologists insisted, does a truly unknown language forever resist such transformations?

Alien tongues could be strange not merely in vocabulary and grammatical rules, but in their semantic swamps and mute cultural or even biological premises. Could even the most inspired programmers, just by symbol manipulation and number-crunching, have cracked ancient Egyptian with no Rosetta Stone?

With the Pluto Project already far over budget, the decision to send Wiseguy along had been hotly contested. The deciding vote was cast by an eccentric but politically astute old skeptic, who hoped to *dis*prove the "bug-eyed monster Rosetta Stone theory" (as he called it) should life unaccountably turn up on Pluto, gambling that his support would bring along the rest of the DIS package—in whose efficacy he firmly and passionately believed. Wiseguy had learned Japanese in five hours; Hopi in seven; Dolphin in two days. It also mastered some of the fiendishly complex, multi-logic artificial grammars generable from an Earth-based mainframe.

The unexpected outcome of six billion dollars and a generation of cyberfolk was simply put: a good translator had all the qualities of a true artificial intelligence. Wiseguy *was* a guy, of sorts. It—or she, or he—had to have cultural savvy *and* blinding mathematical skills. Shanna had long since given up hope of beating Wiseguy at chess, even with one of its twin processors tied off.

She signaled to get the Pluto creature's attention, and while flying-things swooped and auroras danced, the Earthling and the Plutonian stumblingly began to talk.

Wiseguy had been eavesdropping on the radio crosstalk already, and was galloping along. In contrast to the simple radio signals she had first heard, the spoken, acoustic language turned out to be far more sophisticated. Wiseguy, however, dealt not in grammars and vocabularies so much as in underlying concepts, so that Shanna and the Zand only briefly had to go through the "me-Tarzan-you-Jane" stage. Fortunately the Plutonian, for a life form that had no clearly definable brain she could detect, proved a quick study.

She got his proper name first, as distinguished from his identifying signal; *its* name, actually, for the translator established early in the game that these organisms had no gender.

The Zand. But it seemed that the name was also generic, for all of them. Like Earth tribes who named themselves "the people," except that Pluto's individuals also seemed to do the same. They distinguished themselves individually, however, when necessary or socially pleasant. A unique alternative to Earth's selfish individualisms and stifling collectivisms, Shanna thought; the political theorists back home would go wild.

Basic values became clear: Rendezvous, modified by personal territoriality. Self-merge, freely chosen (the concept of "rape" was unknown), with all the zands working communally afterward to care for the young should there luckily occur a Birthing. Respect for age, because it had experienced so much more, tempered by skepticism, because it embroidered that experience—as when telling the young the tale of the raiders from Darkside.

Shanna would scarcely have noticed the splashing and grinding on the beach as other zands began to arrive for Rendezvous, save that the Zand—*her* zand—stopped to count and greet the new arrivals. Her earlier worry about being crunched under a press of huge zand bodies was obviously groundless. This barren patch of rock was now her particular zand's turf, and was respected.

Shanna felt a sharp ache in her lower back, from sitting motionless for so long, and was astounded to realize that nearly four hours had passed. She forced herself to get up, stretch, eat, and drink—none of them easy, in the lander's tiny cabin—and check the instruments.

She was nearing the end of the vehicle's air and fuel reserves. Damn it, she didn't want to quit *now*!

The solution came in a flash. If the big creature's vacuum organ could be clamped over the lander's intake ports, which had probably cooled enough by now to be safe for the Plutonian to touch, she could top out her oxygen and hydrogen tanks from the Plutonian's internal fuel storage organs and stick around for a while.

The Zand took advantage of their work break to hunch up the hillside a short way to feed. On its return, another zand slid up alongside; a courtship preliminary, Shanna guessed.

Tentatively, the newcomer laid its body next to that of the first Zand—which abruptly, even curtly, it seemed to Shanna, rolled away. She laughed aloud. How many Earthmen had she known who would pass up a chance at sex in order to get on with their language lessons?

As the Zand approached the lifecraft, Shanna explained what she wanted. It quickly got the idea, and shortly native-brewed O_2 and H_2 were pouring into Earth-built chambers. Then, refreshed by its mid-morning snack, the Zand began asking *her* the questions, and the first one nearly floored her: "Do you come from Lightgiver?"

Shanna had early realized that in addition to a society, an empirical view of the world, and an epic oral literature, the zands possessed a religion. Agnostic though she was, the discovery moved her profoundly. After all, she thought with a rush of compassion and nostalgia, we started out as sun-worshippers too. Those great lenses on the zands' upper sides, unlike proportionately tiny human eyes, could resolve the point of Sol's light into a disk, and they had drawn what seemed the obvious conclusion.

To the Zand's question, however, she quickly said "No." As soon and as tactfully as possible Shanna got the interchange turned around, so that she was again asking the questions and the Zand answering them.

Their calendar concept of short and long warm-cold cycles intrigued her. Obviously it corresponded with Pluto's rotational day and orbital year, an impressive feat of observation and deduction for a people who lacked a technology. Shanna soon realized, however, that this idea was new to the Zand; that in fact it had learned the information that very planetary day from an untutored genius it referred to as Old One. She pressed it further, and learned the cold arithmetic of which Old One had discoursed while floating over the sea.

The moment she realized those numbers' implication for the future of Pluto, Shanna West, for the first time since she had been a very small child, began to cry.

Don't waste our damn time on tears, Shanna sternly told herself. But she remained silent, truly at a loss for what to say.

Incredibly, the Zand itself intuited her distress and tried to console her: "Do not sad. Lightgiver gives and Lightgiver takes away; bless Lightgiver."

Zands did not use verb forms underlining existence itself—are, is, be—so "sad" became a verb. She wondered what deeper philosophical chasm that revealed. Still, the phrasing was startlingly familiar—the same damned, comfortless comfort Shanna had heard preached at Grandma's funeral. Remembering that moment of loss with a deep inward hurt she forced it away.

After an awkward silence, the Zand said something renderable as "I need leave you for now."

Another zand was peeping out her Zand's personal identification signal, with a slight modification. Both sound communication and radio traffic between the two zands became intense. The shipboard computer did its best to interpret—and Shanna turned the translator off. First things first, and even on Pluto there was such a thing as privacy.

Shanna prepared the lander for lift-off. She hoped its heat of launching, carried through Pluto's frigid air, would add to the sun's thin rays and the inner Oort Cloud's electromagnetic influx and help induce a Birthing. Too bad she could not transmit Wagner's *Liebestod* to the pair, but even Wiseguy could only do so much.

She lingered, held both by scientific curiosity and a newfound affection. Sections of carbon exoskeleton popped forth from the shiny skin of both zands. Jerkily, the carbon-black leaves articulated together into one great sphere. Inside, she knew, the two zands were flowing together as one being. Self-merge.

Shanna punched the firing keys. The lander rose up on its tail of fire. Her eyes were dry now, and her next move was clear: "I've got to talk to Old One."

VII

The Project auditorium was not as festive as the night before, and not nearly as full.

Pluto was gone from the viewscreen, which showed instead a newscast from Earth. Framed by a stock background shot of Red Square, a gaunt Tass functionary was, surprisingly, orating in the old Vyshinsky rant-and-rave style, long since considered gauche in the USSR. WorldScan's fluent Intranslation turned his Russian into almost equally pungent English: "This time the imperial war masters of Wall Street and the Pentagon have truly overreached themselves. To distract the attention of the world's masses and to drum up new financing for their militaristic space program, they have invented a bourgeois fairy tale. Life on Pluto! But this new superstition will not beguile the progressive forces of the world, nor dissuade them from their historic task of building socialism." Mercifully, the pickup cut away from what was doubtlessly much more of the same.

Wall Street and the Pentagon were doing no such thing, Benjamin Rabi ruminated, shifting in his seat in the back row of the auditorium. They weren't saying anything at all about Pluto—and that was worrisome. Just at that moment Hilge Jensen came in and sat down beside him, and on an impulse which quite surprised the Administrator he took her hand. To his still greater surprise her strong surgeon's fingers returned the pressure and she moved closer to him.

With a sigh, the Administrator checked his personal chronometer and let go of Hilge's hand. Nearly 1500 and time for Shanna's next schedule; he'd better get to the platform. He rose and started climbing over people's legs.

Harvell Swain met the Administrator and the doctor halfway down the slanting floor. "Any feedback yet on the stuff you've been putting out?" Ben asked.

"Oh. Christopher Columbus sets foot on last unknown land; Robinson Crusoe looks for Friday? Not much." The PR man stepped close and lowered his voice to a conspiratorial sotto voce: "Matter of fact, nothing at all. The word from Earthside is that Washington agrees with the Russians about Pluto."

As if to underscore Swain's point, World-Scan cut to the floor of the U.S. House of Representatives. A large, loose-limbed youngish man stood by his desk, one foot planted on his chair, one hand waving a sheaf of papers.

"Life on Pluto," the man drawled. *"Life on Pluto?"* he repeated, turning it into an incredulous question. "Just when this House is gettin' ready to vote on that new, gold-plated spaceship that runs on nuke bombs—*another* trillion bucks and more good American lives goin' down the pot—just then, they happen to let us know there's life on Pluto?"

He paused, slapped the papers down on his desk, and shouted, "Mr. Speaker, there ain't no life on Pluto, just like there was none on Titan or any other place but God's green Earth, and I ain't takin' no more of these skin games!"

Rabi struggled for calm, thoughts racing. The Project's own urgencies had distracted him too long from the "real world," as it smugly called itself. The deaths aboard *Proserpina* had reignited an old political prejudice. Space programs had been attacked, off and on, for three-quarters of a century, though rarely this viciously. Somehow, if we didn't go into space, we would get urban renewal—or a balanced budget, if you were on the other side of the political fence. He would have to put out a statement—hell, there wasn't time. The Administrator signaled the tech to pull the newscast and put Pluto back on the screen.

Ben Rabi stepped into the holofocus and waited for the watchers' uneasy rumble of talk to subside. "Ladies and gentlemen, I'll not dignify what you've been seeing and hearing just now by arguing with it. There isn't time right now, and reality speaks for itself."

A few cries of "Hear, hear!" buoyed him. He smiled wryly.

The locals were noisy and loyal. Still, he felt the vast weight of sluggish humanity beyond, a whole swarming planet, half gaunt and angry, the other half grown fat and blurred by its own incessant indulgences. Or maybe they were simply easily distracted, like children addled by complexity.

But powerful children. They would strike swiftly.

The myriad economic webbings that tied Earth to its moon brought stress and friction. Tensions had built for a long time now, and this craziness about Pluto was just frustration blowing off pointless steam.

But it could scald them all. Make a nice, vindictive three-day news item; just the kind of savory bit the networks loved.

It all made weird but plausible sense. Ben had built a reputation for anticipating problems, though he thought of this trait as mostly pure luck. Now he sensed a disaster about to happen and he had damn few tools to work with.

People. In the end that was all you really had. He would have to start preparing now, guessing Earthside's moves.

He gritted his teeth. Seconds had ticked by. What should he say? Keep it bland, unworried.

"Shanna West told us last night that she was going to land on Pluto. Now, I trust, she is back from that epochal journey and is safe on board *Proserpina*. Her next radio schedule was timed to reach us this afternoon, so let's hear what she has to say." He paused. The second hand on the old schoolroomlike wall clock swung up to 3 P.M.

And past it.

And around again.

Nothing came across the six billion kilometers of intervening darkness except the hiss of far stars.

A buzz of disquiet began to rise in the hall. The Administrator covered the situation as well as he could: "It is, of course, quite possible that Astronaut West is still on Pluto. We'll let you know at once if we hear anything more." He signaled the tech to put the newscast back on.

"If Shanna is still on Pluto, she is dead," Hilge Jensen said evenly.

"I wouldn't bet on it," Ben shot back. But in his heart were the chilling words of Pascal: *the eternal silence of these infinite spaces frightens me.*

VIII

1500 GMT at Moonbase One. High noon in Pluto's rotational time, as measured from the place where the Zand had awakened that morning.

Early afternoon by the same measure at Rendezvous, where the great double-sized spheres, starkly black against the gleaming ices, still sheltered most of the zands in the nirvana of Self-merge.

Dead of night on Pluto's far side, where Shanna West flew toward another kind of rendezvous. Behind the lander like a great obedient dog, occasional starlight glinting from its polished upper side, floated *Proserpina*'s largest probe, following her.

Darkness and the deep. Torn by tidal pressure-ridges, the icy wastes of Pluto's night side rolled to the foreshortened horizon. Since there was atmosphere—thicker and denser than anybody had expected—the stars did not show forth as baleful unwinking points; they flickered and glittered as on crisp nights at high altitudes on Earth. Near the magnetic poles, silently swirling blue auroral glow cloaked the hard glitter.

Shanna turned off the lander's interior lights so she could watch. The dashboard chronometer remained lit, insistently reminding her of entropy's inexorable flow.

1505 GMT at Moonbase One. They could have been receiving her third report to the Project now, had she filed one immediately after leaving the Zand.

It was dangerous to have gone off on her own this way, she knew. Risky and downright juvenile. Guilt nagged at her for not having kept the radio schedule. Ben would probably worry himself sick. She was torn between her urge to explore and her duty to the mission, to three dead crewmates. But on leaving the Zand she had met Old One, and that encounter had changed everything.

She had told it a great deal more than she had told the first Zand—about Earth—because she thought it could handle the information load. Old One's intellectual achievement simply staggered her. Here, all rolled into one, was the Aristotle, the Bacon, the Galileo, potentially perhaps the Einstein, of the zand species—with no written language or notational system or even a telescope, much less a computer. To be sure, she realized, the zand philosopher-scientist had the advantage of time; it had lived, after all, more than four hundred Earth years.

Old One had blithely skipped most of the semantic and conceptual preliminaries she had gone through with her first Zand. In fact, the native savant shortly had started communicating directly with Discursive and Integrative System, *Proserpina*'s superbrain—DIS, the Greek equivalent of Pluto, was its entirely appropriate acronym—and Wiseguy, the translator, had ceased to include Shanna in the interchange at all; that would only have slowed them down.

Old One, however—unlike some geniuses Shanna had known on Earth—had tact. It had abruptly halted what must have been for it a heady conversational brew in order to bring her up to date. It knew what she had come direct from Rendezvous to ask; her "vitamin" hypothesis did, after a fashion, fit the facts.

The zands suffered from what amounted to nutritional deficiencies. Analogously to Earth species, they needed trace elements of several kinds for full health and strength, even for survival. The remedy lay, in a sense, close at hand—and in another way frustratingly, tantalizingly far off. That was why Old One had philosophically resigned itself, on the next day-cycle or the next, to die.

Lights frequently streaked across Pluto's somber heavens. Some of them pounded into the ice or plunged into the sea as what Old One called "skystones." Shanna knew whence they came: the cometary Oort Cloud which surrounded the Solar System to a depth of a third of a light-year, but whose inner edge intersected the orbits of Pluto and Neptune. Pluto, nearer the Cloud than Earth and shielded by less atmosphere, was far more vulnerable to hammering by meteoric debris.

The zands' life was thus even more precarious than she had imagined. Only by sheer cosmic accident—or as they would have said, by the mercy of Lightgiver—had a stray comet never pulverized Rendezvous or sent a tidal wave to roll over the zands during their breakfasting or Birthing. Only by another such accident—or miracle—had the Oort Cloud debris back near the Solar System's beginning bombarded the planet in enough quantity to let the organisms that depended on it evolve in the first place, before petering out as the zand civilization dawned. One of those lightning hunches that had often given Shanna a competitive edge during astronaut training suddenly struck her: *evolve? Who said they evolved?* The implications of that were too much for now—she brushed them aside.

Out there in primordial Chaos and ancient Night, in tiny but sufficient quantities, lay the heavy metals and rare earths the zands needed in their food. The practical problem was that many skystones fell into the day's large methane ocean, where at sunset they irrecoverably froze. Or else the skystones ploughed into the cliffs and crevasses on the night side—into which zands never ventured—only to sink into the liquefying surface when that side of the planet in its turn faced the sun.

If a zand should be lucky enough to find the

meteoric material at dawn, before the precious stuff sank into the melting methane sea—or *if* it could dive into the shallows, searching for treasure on the frozen shelf . . . but the chances were so slender. They had so little time.

Shanna reluctantly—for such a mass of knowledge remained untapped in her new-found mentor's mind!—had bidden Old One farewell. She borrowed from the ancient zand's organic oxygen and hydrogen for the lander, and then took off for Darkside. She was going to become a meteor miner.

The big probe, summoned from *Proserpina*'s hold, met her at the atmosphere's edge. The two vehicles descended toward Pluto's nighted surface to search for cometary debris.

Lights. Brimming yellow dots on the upcoming horizon. Not in the sky; on the ice.

A coldness not of Pluto's giving invaded her. Shanna wished she had questioned Old One more fully before charging off this way. Could the zands' tribal epic, of the great raid from Darkside in the distant past, be true?

But there couldn't, strictly speaking, *be* any Darksiders. All of the planet was exposed to the sun in due course as it rotated. Surely "Darksiders" could come out in the zands' own territory after nightfall, while day-living Eaters and Flappers and zands could flourish on "Darkside" when it faced the sun?

As Shanna drove on further into the night, a great, sickly greenish yellow arc rose up before her, blotting out stars—and she thought she had part of her answer.

Charon was synchronous in its orbit—the fat

gray moon hung perpetually above this part of the planet. When the twin worlds swung around into sunlight, Charon—so appropriately named after the ferryman of Hades!—would cast a large shadow. Eclipsed, the tiny sun would give even less warmth than on the opposite hemisphere, and this side of Pluto would be far chillier. Even at high noon here it snowed.

Life filled its appropriate ecological niches, as Darwin had seen in the Galapagos long ago. One half of Pluto, she speculated, was home for the zands; the other was the "Darksiders' " domain.

No, damn it! That wouldn't work. Charon had only started regularly eclipsing the sun within the past half century. Evolution is not *that* swift.

Unless—unless the strange orbital shift was what *brought* the Darksiders out of wherever they hid for most of Pluto's long orbital year?

Two centuries ago, Shanna conjectured, Charon's orbit had similarly moved to screen out the sun. (Why? the nagging inner voice asked. Did that have anything to do with the odd—but natural—radio emissions that the Space Array had discovered? Put that by for now also.)

And then Darkside had raided Rendezvous. The zands, their battle story told them, had barely survived that Gotterdammerung. And this time, Shanna suddenly realized, if the Darksiders moved within the next few Earth hours, they would catch the greater part of the zand nation's effective fighting forces helpless, immobilized in the afterglow of Self-merge.

Warily Shanna edged the lander farther in under Charon's washed-out rays. She examined the breadboard circuitry she had rigged. The kluged job converted a delicate scientific probe into a roistering open-pit miner. One small circuit change—there. Now it was not a raw foods processor but a weapon; literally plowshare into sword.

Shanna's grandmother had dinned "reverence for life"—all life—into her. Could she make this terrible choice, to save the zands? She gritted her teeth. Why, why must first contacts with other cultures *always* turn out this way?

A circle of darkness below, breaking the anemically moonlit landscape, shocked her into full alertness. Quickly she called on *Proserpina*'s computer for data. The temperature differentials DIS could measure, minute to the point of insignificance, dimly sketched for her the walls and floor of a deep pit. Quite patently artificial.

Down at the bottom stood blocky, jointed-limbed Somethings, each outlined in a weird blue argon glow. Ghostly forms moved sluggishly. They were forming into neatly aligned ranks and files, like an army on parade—or a warfleet.

Were they organisms or machines? DIS couldn't tell her without a whole further set of assumptions. Out here, did such distinctions even matter?

On an inspired hunch Shanna asked the

ship's library to search under "Superconductors." Yes—there were plenty of compounds down there rich in copper and oxygen. That made them superconductors at these temperatures. So energy pumped in by the Plutonian electrodynamic weather—riding those voltages trickling in from the Oort Cloud—could be stored indefinitely. No wasteful dissipation of energy reserves in the long sleep times. Then—a swift, sure source of efficient energy.

A half-dozen small hoverers sprang upward, circling within the pit. Blue lights around the regimented ranks dimmed. Zero hour; no more time for dispassionate study.

She hit the controls. The lander danced up and away, maneuvering above the center of the great pit. Shanna took a deep breath. Three humans had died to reach this place. Those were not her fault . . . but the lives below would be. Yet she had to follow her instincts, the deft feel of intuition. Even if she would regret it the rest of her life.

Her thumb touched the special relay she had rigged. The probe dropped like a stone into a well—achingly slow in this world's weaker gravity.

The haywired relay told the probe's rocket nozzles to close, and its fuel tanks to vent into its empty cargo hold. She had simplified an instrument designed for delicate exploration of an alien world . . . into a bomb.

Tensely Shanna counted—God, this hole was *deep*!—and an instant before impact, she hit the probe's cutting torch. The O_2/H_2 mixture promptly exploded.

Pluto shook to the blow of a giant yellow fist. Orange flames blasted out of the pit; the thin air shouted aloud. Steam rolled up out of the Darksiders' ravaged hiding place, condensing at once into water-ice crystals that rattled down in a frigid shower. Debris shot far and wide. A shock wave slammed into the lander—and something solid screeched right through from wall to wall, in and out again. Its passage sounded like a giant's handclap.

Shanna was in her armor—otherwise explosive decompression would have finished her. Earth air screamed out of the lander. Pluto's cold gases sighed in.

She fought the lander's controls; the little vehicle swayed and sank like a drunken express elevator. Deceleration jets sputtered, then coughed out. With a shriek of twisting metal the lander thumped down. Three legs buckled under, canting the deck steeply.

Blood ran down one cheek. Her right shoulder hurt atrociously. But the personal armor for the Pluto mission had been designed to be survivable, and Shanna survived. The silence in the shattered cabin, after so much thunder, seemed eerie. She saw her breath frosting over the faceplate and turned up the armor's heater. It gave a wan warm breath. Air cut her throat. Her legs were already getting numb. She was not, after all, going to be given very much more time.

A pouch near her mouth held medication designed for just such a terminal emergency. No pain, the briefers had told her; a bland taste, drowsiness, and then—nothing.

No, damn it; she just wasn't the suicidal type. With blunt fingers she operated the armor's remote handlers to contact *Proserpina.* She couldn't talk to Moonbase, but the ship could trigger a signal she had long since prearranged, to let them know—

Noise.

Clanking, tearing, cutting, tromping.

A square, bulky helmetlike object, outlined in cold blue light, lurched past the outside viewscreen. Terror—real, little-child fright at monsters in the dark—clutched at Shanna's heart. The Darksiders were here.

The creeping, aching cold fogged her mind. Some small corner of it still knew nonetheless what it was doing. Drunkenly she got the translator up and running. *Outside-direct interface,* she ordered.

"Talk to them," she hoarsely whispered. "Explain . . ."

Talk to them how? the logical, realistic side of her psyche gibed. Even with the simpler zands it had taken hours of practice . . .

A section of wall wrenched away. In through the ragged hole came a many-jointed, metallic-looking limb ending in a lobster claw. It groped along the control board.

"No—don't break anything, *please!*" she cried wildly. As if having heard, the claw stopped. The arm swung across the room and touched her faceplate with a click.

Fast-growing frost crystals framed the claw in an ivory glow.

Tired . . . cold . . . no; mustn't—not yet.

Poking blindly with her stiffening hands, she

worked the handlers and somehow got Wiseguy's attention. "Tell them . . . need warm . . . warm . . ."

Shanna slumped. Her icy armor stung her flesh through her padded jumpsuit. "So wrong . . . about Darksiders . . . So wrong."

She was falling through space, into an endless nighted gulf. The ultimate outrage was that a last lucid spark of awareness was able to watch it happening.

Down . . . down . . . down.

IX

Long, slanting afternoon rays stained the cliffs of Rendezvous in turquoise and pale gold. The thin air rang to the cracking and clanging of scores of round, dark shells as they opened like great eggs.

Old One, hovering over the placid sea just off shore, came alertly out of its meditations. It moved toward a stretch of barren shingle. There its particular young friend—and the zand who currently was the other-of-it in Self-merge—were already drawing apart like giant. slick amoebas.

And there, glistening on the sand between them, feebly stirring, lay no less than seventeen infant zands. A Birthing, and a splendid one.

Harsh cries clashed in the cold air. Flappers, patiently poised above Rendezvous to wait for

Self-merge to end, now folded themselves and arrowed downward.

With quick energy it had not known it still possessed, Old One flipped over. It pointed its after aperture at the sky—and fired.

Hunger-calls turned to screams of dying rage. Blackening Flapper bodies fell to ground. A host of small scavengers raced out of the Eater-shrubbery to feed on the smoking remains.

Baffled, the surviving Flappers circled over the beach, readying to strike again. By this time other zands, who had forgone the bliss of Self-merge in order to stand guardian should there be Birthings, came hurrying into action. A furious, snapping air battle erupted over Rendezvous.

The little new zands below obeyed the genetic impulse imprinted into them. They scrambled down the sterile, foodless stretch of beach, searching for Eaters to give them life-gas. Not finding any, they dove with tiny splashes into the sea.

There a gray scum of marine organisms fed on microscopic crystals of ammonia and carbon dioxide, and exhaled hydrogen, the gas of life. Adult zands flocked in behind them and joined end-to-end in a living wall, fencing off those shallows as a swimming area for the young. One warder on the seaward side cried out as its body took the impact of a Borer. A Flapper darted in, nipped off the parasite's body behind the head, and flapped away.

"Feed the young some of this!" Old One peremptorily commanded, indicating some of the unmeltable blue-gray rocks.

The zand nurturers hastened to obey, catching the small wrigglers and shoving gritty sand-grains into them.

"You also—take some . . ." and Old One scooped and blew some of the harsh, sharp-edged stuff from the beach into the forward orifice of the Zand who was its friend. Then Old One flung into its friend's maw a ration of Eaters. Still groggy after Self-merge, the Zand warbled its gratitude.

With great effort the Zand and its late shell-mate struggled up, singing the first notes of the Hymn of Birthing. All along hillsides and ice-hollows of Rendezvous, other zands joined in thanks and praise to Lightgiver.

But a strange, new sorrow gnawed at Old One. It joined, with the quaverings of age, in the song; but inwardly it wondered—did Lightgiver truly hear?

Old One had long been certain that Lightgiver did not move across the sky; that the world in its day turned toward the bright body in the sky and then away. Putting together its own thinking with what the Earther had said, it now reasoned further—that in the much greater cycle from warm to cold, Lightgiver did not approach and recede from the world. Instead, the world traveled in a great eccentric loop, first closer to the Source of light and life, then away.

So far this was compatible with zand theology and perhaps even strengthened it; Lightgiver was not a wanderer across the sky but the unmoved Center of all. But Lightgiver Itself, the Earther had finally admitted, moved on a still greater track in the sky, to a destination unknown—from which Old One drew the stunning conclusion that Lightgiver was in fact one of those strange bright points in the sky that multiplied at twilight and grew fewer at dawn.

Now, as it listened to its fellow zands sing chorus after triumphant chorus of the Hymn of Birthing, the eldest of the tribe began to understand why the Earther had been reluctant to part with this information. The strong, simple faith the zands had in Lightgiver as the knowing, caring Awakener and Nourisher of all life had carried them through hunger and storms. Through the attacks of Flappers and Borers. Through bitter disappointments of dwindling Birthings. And through much else, for cycle after hard, weary cycle.

With the new knowledge just gained of their world, they might yet prevail. But Old One decided it would not, at this critical time, share with them a further revelation that must surely make them falter and despair. Most of the motive essence that sustained them, the Earther had hinted, did not come from Lightgiver at all.

Actually the Earther, even though it had never known the zands' primordial faith, had acted very much like a follower of Lightgiver's Way. It had given, freely and without question. It had shared sadness and joy. And at the end, for the zands' sake, it had risked its own life and heroically sallied off to Darkside.

Old One did not expect the Earther to return

from Darkside; much imponderable evil lurked there—and greater love had none, said the zand proverb, than to lay down life for one's friends.

But such an equivalency with their own highest values was probably, as yet, far too much to expect the zand folk as a whole to accept. So the ancient philosopher of the zands, summoning some of the strength that had waned with age, sang lustily.

To its deepest, most honest self, however, Old One added: *Nevertheless, it moves.*

X

Shanna woke.

She hadn't expected to. But none of the kinds of afterlife she had ever visualized included lying naked in a warm nutrient bath.

The green, acrid, medicinal-smarting fluid drained out beneath her. She sat up.

Not a mark on her; not even, so far as she could tell by feel, a facial scratch suffered in the crash. And internally she felt fine. Ravenous, but great.

Proserpina's life-support program was passing a test nobody on Pluto Project had ever imagined.

And then the realities hit her.

It wasn't just the ship and the wise artificial intelligence that ran it which had performed this miracle.

The Darksiders had kept her alive. *Or brought her back from the dead?*

The Darksiders had taken her off Pluto and up to her ship. That meant they had space travel—or bodies that could travel through space.

The Darksiders, without damage to the ship, had delivered her inside. That meant an order of intelligence at least as good as Earth's; and judging from their ability to deal with her alien and, to them, previously unknown metabolism—probably a good deal better.

Shanna's mind reeled at this enormous shift in perspective. Now she could better understand how Old One must have felt.

Then, as she stood to climb out of the tank, a triumphant wave of elation surged through her and pushed all other thoughts aside. *Hooray! I'm alive!*

Shanna set the adjoining shower cubicle for a full, vigorous needle-spray and stepped inside. She took it happily until the water recycler blinked to warn her that she was overusing the facility. Then she let a gush of cold water pour down on her for several seconds before shutting it off. Rather than activate the air-dryer, she stepped out, tingling, and wrapped herself in a huge bath towel. *Now you should get some soup into you,* her grandmother would have said at this point. So Shanna did.

Afterward she programmed the autochef for one of its most elaborate meals; the ingredients, recipe, and computer routine had been a farewell gift from the French scientists on Phobos. As preparation began, Shanna shrugged herself into a fresh coverall. Some astronauts and cosmonauts she had known, when not actually working, adjusted temperature and humidity controls and floated around in their cabins nude. Shanna, however, had worn clothes every ship-day for much the same reason British colonial officers in the old days, even in the steaming tropics, had donned full formal dress for dinner each evening. It was a connection with civilization.

The autochef signaled that the first course was served. Shanna turned up the audio and put on the Brahms *German Requiem*—music which, despite its sometimes lugubrious words, seemed to her actually one of the most joyous, life-affirming works ever composed.

"Here on earth we have no continuing abode. . ." Her thoughts strayed from the music back to Pluto. The Darksiders—many of whom she had just killed—had nevertheless saved her life. Yet they had also, if legend be trusted, viciously attacked the zands a long Plutonian year ago, and she was certain that only her crude bomb had stopped them from doing it again.

How to judge?

She was, in her own origins, American. Would an alien outsider judge America's performance by My Lai and Wounded Knee or by Lincoln and Jefferson?

What kind of consciousness—what kind of ethics—operated with a circulatory system whose medium was liquid nitrogen?

Or had she hallucinated the whole encounter with Darkside?

Enough of *that* nonsense! She jumped up and began to search the ship for evidence of the alien visit, letting Brahms follow her from compartment to compartment. Quickly and disconcertingly she found it: a neat hole, cut all the way through the hull, and an equally neat patch of a dull reddish material Shanna did not know.

The breach had been made mere meters from the life support tanks (*my God, do they know our ship blueprints too?*). Between the patched bulkhead and tank compartment the deck was scratched and scored, as if something had dragged a heavy machine through. A faint tang of ammonia hung in the air.

She raced hand-over-hand up one level, to the main computer console. A light winked at her imperiously from one of the monitors. Input for you from DIS, Shanna. Read me!

The music ended. Shanna looked at the chronometer. 1700 GMT; nearing the end of the Pluto mission's third Earth day.

Two radio schedules missed; Ben and Dr. Jensen must be frantic. She could not yet face playing back whatever worried, subtly reproachful messages they meanwhile might have sent to her.

However, twenty minutes from now Ben's voice would reach *Proserpina* for their next radio schedule . . . twenty minutes Shanna would need to find the essence of what DIS had learned about Darkside—and do some hard, serious, antistereotypical thinking.

Too soon, the musical chime rang. Ben's voice came in: "Shanna, if you can hear me, I'll make it short. I want you to in-load the course corrections you're now receiving. Leave Pluto orbit at once, on course for Moonbase One.

"It's time to come home, kid. We've got troubles here—big troubles." And the message ended.

Ben always called her "kid." Well, she *had* been a kid when she sailed blithely off to Pluto. Losing her three crewmates had been a horrible rite of passage. But only when she had struck Pluto's icy surface and known for the first time her own mortality, Shanna decided, had she really begun to grow up. She activated her voice channel and began to speak.

XI

Benjamin Rabi was used to working late; it went with the job. Dinner had been synthetics on a tray, scarcely touched. Hilge Jensen had come in, given him a relaxing back rub with her wonderfully strong hands, and left. She had her own urgent work to do.

The crumpled printout still lay on one corner of the desk. He knew what it said: PROJECT PLUTO OFFICIALLY TERMINATED 2400 HOURS TODAY YOUR TIME. YOUR REPLACEMENT NOW EN ROUTE ETA MOONBASE ONE 2300.

When it came, Ben had stormed, raged, cursed—but only in the privacy of his office. He had made holophone calls to the few key people who had to be told. Then, puffing furiously on the first of many cigars, he had turned from the desk to his message console and resumed feeding the huge backlog of Pluto data to Earth—before anyone down there could order him not to.

The desk communicator startled him: "Administrator Vandermeer is here, sir."

So soon? Automatically Rabi started to put out the current cigar, then thought better of it. "Send him in," he said.

Hobart Vandermeer, briefcase in hand, stepped carefully over the threshold. He was not alone. Two beefy look-alikes in expensive business suits a size too small for them came in and flanked him, stolid and narrow-eyed.

"You're early." Deliberately Ben blew a cloud of smoke. In twenty-forties First World etiquette the gesture was so rude as to border on the obscene.

Administrator Vandermeer ignored the insult. "I came early to help ease the transition—wind up your paperwork, arrange for your passage Earthside, and the like. I'm sure you understand the sensitivity of this matter. By midnight I expect we'll have things all wrapped."

Ben remained silent.

"Do you need help clearing out your desk, sorting files, and so on?"

"I've done all that."

"Your personnel will be reporting back to Washington for reassignment. I can help speed their clearances—"

"They will *not*, with very few exceptions. Moonbase One has been these people's home for five, in some cases ten or twelve years. They've no intention of going back to Earth, ever. Many of them can't, for gravitational cardiac reasons."

The amiable manner faded. "Listen up, Rabi. *Pluto Project is finished.* After tonight it won't even be a nameplate on that door. If you give me any trouble on this, I am authorized to place you under arrest."

Vandermeer nodded; one of the hulks smoothly moved over and stood behind the desk. "If it turns out you are a party to the Pluto life fraud, you will doubtless do time anyway." Rabi's official replacement smiled tightly. "You have ordered Astronaut West to return to Earth, of course."

"I told Shanna at our last radio schedule to start back, yes. You'll need to have a landing crew here to receive *Proserpina*, and to send up course correction data, give advance warning of solar flares . . ."

"Pluto Project closes down *now*," Vandermeer interrupted.

Why, the incredible bastard! Was he actually willing to let Shanna die in space, just to save a few bucks? No; that wasn't the point, Ben knew in a sudden, ugly moment of insight. Certain Earthside elements wouldn't be at all upset if the lone survivor of that design failure never returned. To them, Shanna's eventual testimony before an investigating committee—or grand jury—could be embarrassing.

"Have you considered that you are jeopardizing the only ship of its kind, worth billions, not to mention the R and D? I don't think Congress is going to like that too well." Keep him talking, Ben thought. Get them focused on the argument.

"Congress wants nothing more to do with Pluto. It was a *vote* by Congress, called into emergency secret session when you put out that first cock-and-bull story about hydrogen-breathing Plutonians, that sent me here."

For once, Benjamin Rabi was absolutely at a loss for words.

"I am sorry for any, uh, inconvenience this may cause Astronaut West," the new Administrator half apologized. "I am authorized to inform you, strictly in confidence, that this policy is in large part the result of high-level—*very* high-level—direct conversations between the United States and the Soviet Union. These have been going on for many months, but the Pluto rendezvous precipitated matters."

Ben remembered that plausibly hostile Tass man, and marveled at officialdom's capacity for cynicism. Vandermeer's tone became portentous and didactic: "Both governments have now agreed that an absolute ban on further movement into space is essential, until we solve more urgent problems."

So that was it; after all these years, helped along by the latest, heartbreaking *Challenger*-style disaster, the enemies of Apollo had won. It sounded, in one sense, downright statesmanlike: end the decades-old Star Wars syndrome; "build down" the most lethal of the orbiting hardware; then spend the money thereby saved on literacy and health and nutrition, buying goodwill for the First and Second Worlds in the Third. It would at least be a cheaper form of U.S.-USSR competition than the resources- and brains-draining alternative. Politically feasible because both publics had become blasé toward their governments' 180-degree policy turns; militarily practicable because Soviet and American aerospace commands, mind-locked from many long years of preparing against each other, had fallen into the hangup—Civil War buffs called it the "General McClellan syndrome"—of never having *quite* enough hardware or troops to move, strike, act. So they decided to do nothing.

Ben's lips compressed with anger. "You *really* think you can just call it all off?"

"I *know* we can, mister," Vandermeer said tightly.

"Think the Chinese and Japanese will buy your boycott?"

"We'll bring diplomatic pressure."

"And they'll sneak around you."

"Not if we—"

"The Asians will steal the whole damn Solar System while we're sitting on our thumbs!"

"I don't think you need to worry about issues you don't understand," Vandermeer said with haughty arrogance.

Ben had been counting the seconds. How long could he keep them focused on his anger, so they ignored his desk panel of suddenly flashing lights? Just a bit more . . .

He said bitterly, "I sure as hell hope you've got your goddamn paperwork in order."

"More than paperwork, mister." Vandermeer smiled, a thin, bloodless crease. "I've deployed two dozen technicians at your link points."

"Huh?" Ben blinked, though he had known about the two dozen before they ever set foot here. He had learned which vital points they were to hold, and how.

"I've got your comm and power network already rolled up."

"Damn!" Ben tried to make himself look angry, frustrated. Not easy when he wanted to laugh.

In the end, all you really had was people. And each of Vandermeer's two dozen had walked into a trap. The teeth were closing right now. The flashing console meant that there were casualties, trouble.

Count the damage later. Once the two dozen were herded into detention cells.

Vandermeer smirked. "We've got you."

"Just out of curiosity," Ben asked, suddenly calm, "what about the data?"

Puzzled, Vandermeer said, "What does that—"

"Shanna sent us plenty—and it's now with the BBC, *Tokyo Times, New York Times*—you name it." He didn't even mention the river of information still pouring into the facility this very moment, flickering grayly on the wall screens.

Vandermeer's answer shocked him: "Your 'data,' so-called, are no doubt the result of the spaceship onboard computer's *very* clever graphics. Did you think special effects would make us forget Titan? We are talking, Mr. Rabi, about conspiracy to defraud the United States taxpayer. It is my understanding that the Justice Department already has this matter under investigation and is preparing charges."

The squawk box broke into the soon-to-be-ousted Project Director's dark thoughts. "Mr. Administrator? We're ready to come in and take away your desk now."

Ben's voice was calm, but his big body tensed. "Yes; come on in." The furniture movers filed in through the door; three men, two women. A typically, bureaucratically overpadded work detail, it would seem to Vandermeer, but not excessively so . . .

Two of the men jumped Ben's guard while one of the women was pushing over his chair. Ben knocked his head pretty hard on the floor, but at least it was out of the way when the handgun the mug had been packing roared. The other man and woman pinioned the second guard's arms.

Rabi's head was ringing. He came up in a rush and got his replacement by the throat. "These," he said good-naturedly after catching his breath, "are members of the Moonbase One Volunteer Self-Defense Force. I organized it this afternoon. In this town, we've *all* got a stake in space, Mr. Vandermeer."

Vandermeer was shaken but he said sharply, "If I don't report in at midnight, they'll send in the Marines!"

"I think not." That *had* to be a desperation bluff; Earth's economy no longer could survive without the asteroid minerals and Moonbase's know-how and facilities for working them. Earther substitutes just couldn't hack it, and

Moonbasers weren't about to work at the point of a gun.

"Take them away," said Ben Rabi briskly, "and put them on the next shuttle to Earth. As apologists always say, they were only doing their job."

Whistling out his breath in a great whoosh of relief as the ill-assorted group left, Ben relit his cigar and took several long drags. Then he pinched it out—he would, after all, be seeing Hilge Jensen soon—and headed for the Project Auditorium.

Ben took a seat in the audience with Hilge. He was surprised and pleased that the place was packed. Not with newspeople; most such types had gone back Earthside to cover vividly picturable fires and mini-revolutions.

Harvell Swain, nervous and apologetic, predictably had quit. ("It's my career, Mr. Administrator. They say if I don't cool it with this Pluto stuff I've been sending for you, now that it's being exposed as a scam, they'll blacklist me from New York to Tokyo.")

In compensation, all the off-duty scientists, maintenance workers, hydroponics farmers, lunar landvehicle drivers, and other Moonbase One folk had turned out in force. Some had brought their small children to hear what rumor said would be Shanna West's last transmission from Pluto orbit before starting the long voyage home.

And at 2245 it came.

"Ben, Dr. Jensen—anyone else listening out there—I'm back from Pluto."

Relief filled the Administrator that she had

been there to answer at all. But then he did some mental subtracting: between his own message summoning Shanna home and the start of her reply, she would have had only five minutes to react. That, knowing Shanna, was a bit worrisome. And, sure enough, her next line was a blow to the body:

"Ben . . . in answer to what you asked me to do, I'm not coming back to Moonbase One, or Earth. Not now, and maybe not ever."

A sudden uproar, quickly shh'd into silence by people who wanted to hear.

"We've got an endangered species up here," Shanna went on.

Hell, kid, Ben silently retorted, we've got one down here too, and we're it.

"Two of them told me their story while I was down on the planet. I backloaded what the translator was doing up to *Proserpina*—no great trick for DIS—and all of that information is on its way back to you now. What I didn't know then, and so couldn't tell you, was that another life form exists out here. The Darkside Plutonians turned out to have intelligence that is superior to ours. That changes everything."

She told them—modestly, yet exuberantly—the whole tale of her heroic journey into Pluto's aurora-lighted night.

"Will Earth buy that?" Rabi asked Jensen, almost inaudibly.

"Not if they didn't buy her other reports. *I* didn't, you remember, until I saw those close-up images with my own eyes."

"Uh huh."

Ignorance is Strength-*credo quia impossible.* There is no life on Pluto.

"They are utterly strange," Shanna's voice resonated in the crowded, hushed hall. "Even DIS is having a hard time making sense out of the data, but we've figured one thing out, at least. The Darksiders are not native to Pluto at all. They didn't evolve a biology that could go with this planet's chemistry. Instead, I think, they shifted Charon's orbit—in order to make Pluto's daytime under the satellite's shadow more comfortable for them.

"They come from the Oort Cloud. That much I'm sure of.

"Pluto is, for them, a great experiment. By deliberately inputting greater energy than the planet's own low-level ecology had available, they have *evolved* a sentient native Plutonian life form—the zands. Simple ohmic heating wasn't enough; they had to apply the planet's electrodynamically derived AC directly to the 'foodrocks' the native animals consume—and their interference with Charon's orbit has messed up that process. These beautiful auroras are the wastage of the experiment, which may well be failing.

"About three centuries ago, the Darksiders culled the zand colony of unwanted genetic traits. The zands remember it as a battle, with terror and pride, in their folklore. A cold-blooded Darwinian pruning operation, and yes—I'm having real trouble with the ethics of that.

"The Darksiders themselves—or Oort Clouders—run on straight DC electricity. They've developed the zands to bridge the gap, using electrically generated *chemical* energy—for the ultimate purpose of colonizing inward. Toward the sun. Toward us. *We* are *their* frontier. And they are ours.

"So I can't come back to Earth. Not yet, anyhow. What happened to me on Pluto was a First Contact, and a very strange one—I zapped them, then they saved my fool neck. Figure that one out. And now—now, as the only human in these parts, I'm sort of elected our ambassador to Outside. Somehow I've got to open negotiations with them. Or would you like the next contact to take the form of a rip-roaring interplanetary war?"

Benjamin Rabi saw destiny wrapping itself around his protegée like a shroud. "Shanna, it's not worth it," he said softly, and beside him Hilge Jensen said: "Shut up. You know it is."

For the first time the young, confident voice from space wavered. "I'm making this decision sound easy. It's not; I'm not that heartless. It's going to be lonely. And there were other things I'd hoped to do . . . I'll keep on making our schedules, unless Pluto moves out beyond intelligible radio range. But it won't be the same.

"Talk to me, Ben; Dr. Jensen. You're really all I've got back there." A long pause, then: "Good-bye," a quickly choked-off sob, and afterward only the rumble of interstellar noise.

They did talk to Shanna, long and tenderly. Later—much later—Ben, sprawled out, at Jensen's insistence, in the one comfortable chair in her spartan quarters, let the crisis emotions begin to drain away. Surely, he mused, *somebody* Earthside—the French? the Indians?—would analyze DIS's data on Plutonian life and perceive that it had to be true. If the Russians and Americans were really serious about disarming Earth's skies, they could release thousands of redundant nukes for Orion-drive spacecraft. Someone could voyage again to Pluto, much more swiftly than *Proserpina.* And then the Oort Cloud . . .

"She's much deeper than we ever gave her credit for," said Hilge, softly.

Her words jarred Ben's mental train onto another track. "Yeah . . . that Grandma of hers must have really been something."

"It's *not* all genetic, and you know it!" Jensen snapped. "She probably found out early in life that most of her friends just didn't share her intellectual curiosity. Not even here at Moonbase—and that led her to feel somewhat solitary, even when with others."

Yes, Ben reflected, and that personal situation clearly paralleled the world's—a few people trying to press on and learn, and a great many who didn't see the need . . .

"What will you do now, Benjamin?"

"I dunno—run for mayor of Moonbase One, I suppose. We're de facto independent now, though neither we nor Earth will be saying so for a while. We really ought to change the name of this damn town—Moonburg, or Luna Una, or Selenopolis, or even Artemisia, after the Greek goddess of the moon."

"I suppose. But first let's go have dinner at

the Old Terran Inn. We won't be getting any more Earthside, dirt-grown food for quite a long time."

Ben grinned. The classic story of the parents—proxy parents, in their case—who are unable really to get together until the offspring leaves the nest . . .

"I thought you'd never ask."

XII

Cold sunset stained Rendezvous in palest alpenglow. The icy mountainsides lay clean-picked, save for the fine dusting of Eater spores that had settled when the afternoon air began to cool. Out at sea the massed zands, thirty-five hundred strong, sang the Hymn of Day's Departure. The music soared—a multipart canon. As each small group of zands singing their part came to the song's end it would break away from the larger choir, its members dispersing over the sea.

The Zand swam sturdily toward the setting sun. Lightgiver's rays now streamed out from a veil of storm clouds, and the sea riffled with a rising wind. It had lingered too long, the Zand feared. To be caught afloat when the falling temperature irreversibly triggered its Night-change could be fatal. Already the Borers had vanished into the freezing deep, and the Flappers were gone.

And the Zand had much to live for now. Its young—all of whom had survived the persistent attacks from the sky—were quick, eager to learn, zestful. Its friend Old One had shed its customary gloom and seemed determined now to live into another day, and many more.

Clouds rolled up, towering into the sky, obscuring Lightgiver. A freezing blast from Darkside brought the first whirling, spiky crystals of snow.

The Zand decided to gamble some of its precious fuel reserves. Lifegas and burngas ignited, and it soared steeply up from the freezing ocean. Far off, looming against the oncoming storm, rose the peak where it had spent its early morning recovery-time. The Zand drove on hard through the rapidly cooling air.

Snow was blowing in blinding gusts when the Zand reached its chosen retreat for the night, and it nearly crashed into the crag. Sea level had dropped precipitously as the surface fluid froze, shrank in volume, and sank.

Quickly now the Zand drew in masses of the new, loose snow and blew it over the foodrock that would again, as last night, serve as its cache; foodrock which, it noted with satisfaction, was noticeably darkened in color by a blanket of freshly formed Eater spores.

The field of black, night-ready spores was broken, a zand's length down the slope, by an irregularly shaped mass not made of ice. Lightgiver be praised! The heavenly Provider had sent the Zand a skystone. And Old One had taught it, late that day, how needful the skystone-stuff was for life. Carefully the Zand moved the object up to the edge of the cache and covered it also with snow.

The Zand did not see through the blizzard's dancing curtains the small, smooth sphere which had guided that skystone down so that it would land on the world gently, without the usual ice-shattering explosion of hot vapor.

Nor did it know that the Earther it had met that day was at that moment alertly monitoring the little probe, drawing it away from Pluto's weak, icy grip. Shanna's meteor mining, done cautiously over at the planet's present dawn zone, had gone well. And the Darksiders had not interfered.

The Zand settled into the big sleep. It felt a last crackling surge of energy as a current ran down from the sky and found waiting conductivity in the nearby rock. Currents flowed, storing energy within its intricate chemical balance. Though this voltage spike came from immensely far away, in thin trickles of electrons streaming across magnetic fields, to the Zand it simply came from the sky in a prickly, delightful gust. All such gifts were from Lightgiver, it thought, and as it ebbed into restful calm, it issued one last humble prayer of thanks.

XIII

Shanna West sighed and stretched in the spaceship's comfortable pilot chair. The lander was a wreck, but *Proserpina*'s resources could put it back together. Meanwhile the sole remaining probe functioned with grace and precision. And so would she.

Proserpina—Pluto's bride—had a mother named Ceres, goddess of the growing grain (whence the word "cereal"). The daughter ended up stuck in the Underworld six months out of every year, which was the way the ancients poetically explained when to get their crops in, and when to plant again. Shanna, as she helped the zands bring in their harvest, did not want to be similarly mythologized. Consequently, she wouldn't communicate directly with Pluto's natives again, at least not yet. They were going to have a severe enough intellectual revolution as it was—and the price of progress, often, is pain. Let them thank Lightgiver, not the Earth interloper, for this manna from heaven.

Strange, wasn't it, how human and zand music, religion, and ways of caring so often paralleled each other. Maybe it really was a uni-, not a multiverse . . . and maybe (arrogant thought, from a kid?) she could introduce into Darkside ethics the revolutionary notion that other sapients, even if less bright than oneself, ought to be treated not as means but as ends.

Speaking of ends and means, Earth's self-appointed diplomat reflected, she had leverage; *Proserpina* possessed physical capabilities even the Darksiders did not, which she could give or withhold.

Careful there, girl.

"Sleep well," Shanna breathed. Now the hard part began. Her fingers danced over the probe controls. The little globe bobbled and bowed, then shot off toward the Darksiders' domain, now enjoying its pallid day.

Shanna West—alone in a world of unrelentingly hostile cold and ominous dark—was, without noticing it, happy. She could take comfort and companionship from the fact that this last outpost of the sun had, however improbably, harbored life.

And all the smug scientists had been wrong, deeply wrong. Life *was* possible out here. Some guiding hand had stitched together low-temperature chemistry and the tenuous energies of electron flow, knitting a gossamer, lively web. Shanna mused about the lives she had blasted to oblivion, so quick in her certainty. Had those dim forms been truly alive? Definitions, her grandmother once said, had to be like a fat man's belt: big enough to cover the subject but elastic enough to allow for change. Out here life clung to the last vestiges of possible chemistry. And she was sure, now, that evolution alone could not have forged such an intricate ecology, not even in the four billion years Pluto had spun. The things in the pit were not forged from nature's relentless mill, for they did not know anger. They had not wreaked vengeance on her when they had the chance. Instead, they had saved her. For a moment, Shanna pictured the Darksiders at the opposite extreme, as saints; but that, she knew instinctively, was also wrong.

They were, finally, constructions. Not machines, perhaps, but something that stretched the definition of life and probably broke it. The Darksiders were agents of something larger, dispassionate. But what?

Pluto orbited at the very verge of that realm where chemical reactions could proceed with sluggish intent. Beyond here lay a black abyss in which the seemingly fragile bonds between molecules would not crack before the weightless hail of sunlight. In that kingdom only electricity could race and flow, to bring motive meaning from the potentials and gravid capacitances that hung in the vast vacant spaces. Gossamer-thin sheets of electrons drifted silently before the subtle tugs of inductances, in circuits that light itself could barely span in a full day.

Chemistry yielded here to the rule of electrodynamics, which proceeded only a tiny fraction slower than light. Intelligence set free from molecular torpidity could dash across the immensity unchecked by all but the gritty limits of matter's innate resistance.

Something had made use of these truths, some brooding intelligence hitherto unsuspected . . . though the laws had been known to humanity since their discovery in the nineteenth century by people seeking to heat and light their shadowy homes. For some reason the forces out there had conducted an experiment on this little dab of rock and ice, blending the two sources of animation.

What's more, the experiment was still young. What had made it happen *now*? The prospect of Earth's incursion into this bitterly cold place? Perhaps the entire experiment was itself a strange form of communication.

And the Old One . . . How had it learned so much? Superior intelligence? But what had selected for such wit and insight, out here? Where was the evolutionary pressure?

No. She had a gut suspicion that centuries ago, when Old One was young, something began a process of subtle tutoring. And before that, a process of deep, cerebral manipulation among that zand's foreparents.

Otherwise, how could one zand, unaided, have forged so far in explaining their bitter realm? That implied some agency had begun

Old One's education long before humanity even knew the outermost planets existed.

And to what end? Shanna looked outward at the unyielding black and wondered what huge surprises waited there . . . and how long they would be in coming.

And down among the howling winds in the gathering gloom of twilight, with methane snow mounding its night-shielded form, the Zand slept on.

Afterword

Pluto was the lord of the underworld, a dark and forbidding place. So, too, the planet—since its discovery in 1930, we have learned little about it. The Grand Tour mission which would have carried a probe to Pluto by now died, the victim of 1970s budget cuts. So we gathered scanty data about the vast realm at the edge of our solar system. Until the late 1980s, that is.

We now know much more, not because of a flyby mission or great advances in telescopes, but because Pluto has a moon. Discovered in 1978 as a bulge in Pluto's tiny image, Charon happens to orbit in a plane which lines up with Earth once ever 124 years. The eclipse season came in the late 1980s. Had we found the moon only a dozen years later, we would have missed the chance to see it repeatedly pass across Pluto's face. Making such observations permitted astronomers to make comparisons between the planet and moon, greatly advancing our knowledge.

Pluto is tiny indeed for a planet. It is only 2300 kilometers (1400 miles) in diameter, while Charon is 1300 kilometers wide. Seven of the moons in the solar system are larger than Pluto, including our own.

Charon is half as big as Pluto, and some astronomers call the pair a double-planet system. (Our moon is one fourth the size of Earth.) Unlike our moon, Charon revolves about Pluto at exactly the same rate that Pluto rotates, so that the same hemispheres of the worlds always face each other. This is a more rigid system than our own, for someone standing on our moon would see the whole Earth turn. On Charon, one sees only one face of Pluto.

Comparing the spectra from the two dim dots of light permitted astronomers to discern much about the chemistry there. Pluto has great polar caps of methane ice. In Pluto's wan summer this ice may sublime into the thin atmosphere. This chemically reducing "air" may resemble the soup in which Earthly life began.

Apparently the large moon Charon is covered mostly by water ice. Pluto is just big enough to have separated out a rocky core, and holds its methane gas atmosphere with a gravitational pull only a few percent of Earth's. A woman weighing 160 pounds on Earth would weigh only eight pounds there and could jump twenty feet in the air.

Methane doesn't freeze until the temperature drops to nearly 200 degrees below zero

Celsius. The sun is about 900 times fainter than on Earth, so it looks like what it is—a star. It shares the sky with other stars, ten million times more bright but still pointlike and distant.

On such a cold, dark world life seems impossible. The methane atmosphere (called "swamp gas" on Earth) could provide chemical cycling, but what would drive the ecosphere?

Such questions would only occur to fans of the old pulp stories, which routinely infested every planet with gaudy monsters. Paul Carter, noted historian of the pulps and much other cultural iconography, wondered if these new aspects of Pluto allowed a bit of freewheeling speculation. He wrote a story using some of the new data, but found the plausibility a bit thin. In 1987 I met him at the Eaton conference on science fiction criticism at the University of California at Riverside. He had done his homework, even to the point of visiting the Lowell Observatory in Flagstaff, Arizona. He saw there the blink comparator used by Clyde Tombaugh to discover Pluto. But he couldn't think of a way that wan sunglow could animate a Plutonian plot.

When he asked me for advice I tried to work out a possible scheme. It seemed delicious to make plausible what had for so long seemed utterly impossible. (Though Larry Niven had made superconducting beings dwell there, back in the 1960s.) The similarity of the reducing atmosphere to early Earthly conditions tweaked my imagination. In mulling over possibilities I didn't actually attain plausibility, but I did avert impossibility by a hair.

My solution is farfetched, of course. The methods come from some work I was doing at the time on electrodynamic methods of driving astrophysical processes at our galactic center. I parlayed the scraps of data being gathered then about Pluto into a picture of a supercold ecosphere where chemistry isn't the only source of energy. This isn't unknown; we discovered from a Voyager flyby that the upper atmosphere of Uranus is quite warm, apparently heated by the rapid rotation of its magnetic fields. In a very real sense, the magnetic fields that fill space can deliver energy to planets. The farther from the sun, the more relatively important such mechanisms can be, compared with sunlight. But was that enough to kindle a working biosphere? I added another agency, just to be sure.

The story of planetary exploration has been rare for decades, hemmed in by hard facts. It was a genuine pleasure to write one in collaboration with a writer who himself began working in the Golden Age of the 1940s. Thus we've kept a certain air of that pulp era, making the story a bit more dramatic than the hard-nosed styles of today. We wrote it for fun, but with an eye cocked toward the unyielding facts.

—Gregory Benford
March 1989

THE TOR DOUBLES

Two complete short science fiction novels in one volume!

☐	53362-3 55967-3	A MEETING WITH MEDUSA by Arthur C. Clarke and GREEN MARS by Kim Stanley Robinson	\$2.95 Canada \$3.95
☐	55971-1 55951-7	HARDFOUGHT by Greg Bear and CASCADE POINT by Timothy Zahn	\$2.95 Canada \$3.95
☐	55952-5 55953-3	BORN WITH THE DEAD by Robert Silverberg and THE SALIVA TREE by Brian W. Aldiss	\$2.95 Canada \$3.95
☐	55956-8 55957-6	TANGO CHARLIE AND FOXTROT ROMEO by John Varley and THE STAR PIT by Samuel R. Delany	\$2.95 Canada \$3.95
☐	55958-4 55954-1	NO TRUCE WITH KINGS by Poul Anderson and SHIP OF SHADOWS by Fritz Leiber	\$2.95 Canada \$3.95
☐	55963-0 54302-5	ENEMY MINE by Barry B. Longyear and ANOTHER ORPHAN by John Kessel	\$2.95 Canada \$3.95
☐	54554-0 55959-2	SCREWTOP by Vonda N. McIntyre and THE GIRL WHO WAS PLUGGED IN by James Tiptree, Jr.	\$2.95 Canada \$3.95

Buy them at your local bookstore or use this handy coupon:
Clip and mail this page with your order.

Publishers Book and Audio Mailing Service
P.O. Box 120159, Staten Island, NY 10312-0004

Please send me the book(s) I have checked above. I am enclosing \$________
(please add \$1.25 for the first book, and \$.25 for each additional book to cover postage and handling. Send check or money order only—no CODs.)

Name ____________________

Address ____________________

City ____________________ State/Zip ____________________

Please allow six weeks for delivery. Prices subject to change without notice.

THE BEST IN SCIENCE FICTION

☐	54989-9	STARFIRE by Paul Preuss	$3.95
☐	54990-2		Canada $4.95
☐	54281-9	DIVINE ENDURANCE by Gwyneth Jones	$3.95
☐	54282-7		Canada $4.95
☐	55696-8	THE LANGUAGES OF PAO by Jack Vance	$3.95
☐	55697-6		Canada $4.95
☐	54892-2	THE THIRTEENTH MAJESTRAL by Hayford Peirce	$3.95
☐	54893-0		Canada $4.95
☐	55425-6	THE CRYSTAL EMPIRE by L. Neil Smith	$4.50
☐	55426-4		Canada $5.50
☐	53133-7	THE EDGE OF TOMORROW by Isaac Asimov	$3.95
☐	53134-5		Canada $4.95
☐	55800-6	FIRECHILD by Jack Williamson	$3.95
☐	55801-4		Canada $4.95
☐	54592-3	TERRY'S UNIVERSE ed. by Beth Meacham	$3.50
☐	54593-1		Canada $4.50
☐	53355-0	ENDER'S GAME by Orson Scott Card	$3.95
☐	53356-9		Canada $4.95
☐	55413-2	HERITAGE OF FLIGHT by Susan Shwartz	$3.95
☐	55414-0		Canada $4.95

Buy them at your local bookstore or use this handy coupon:
Clip and mail this page with your order.

Publishers Book and Audio Mailing Service
P.O. Box 120159, Staten Island, NY 10312-0004

Please send me the book(s) I have checked above. I am enclosing $________
(please add $1.25 for the first book, and $.25 for each additional book to cover postage and handling. Send check or money order only—no CODs.)

Name ________________________

Address ________________________

City ____________ State/Zip ____________

Please allow six weeks for delivery. Prices subject to change without notice.